KW-326-849

NEXT STOP ROMANCE: A STORY OF OLD BELFAST

An adventure romance story
set in 1900s Belfast

Hugh Bradley

Copyright © 2022 Michael McDermott

All rights reserved

The characters and events portrayed in this book are fictitious.
Any similarity to real persons, living or dead, is coincidental and
not intended by the author.

No part of this book may be reproduced, or stored in a retrieval
system, or transmitted in any form or by any means, electronic,
mechanical, photocopying, recording, or otherwise, without
express written permission of the publisher.

ISBN: 9798357624765

Cover design by: Jaide Bradley
Library of Congress Control Number: 2018675309
Printed in the United States of America

For Hugh, Charlotte, Charlie and Margaret

CONTENTS

FOREWORD

'Next Stop Romance' is a love story wrapped in a history lesson. The story, originally titled 'A Sinn Feiner's Romance', was written by my grandfather, Hugh Bradley, around 1950 at his home in Woodside, Queens. The manuscript sat for years in my family home on Long Island and finally in my own home until I was encouraged to publish it by my cousin Conor in Belfast.

The story is set primarily in the Ardoyne area of North Belfast where Hugh Bradley lived and takes place in Ireland from 1905 through 1921 when Irish Nationalism was on the rise. It is a story by a man who was a participant in the events of which he writes. The main character in the story, Art, is the same age as the author and no doubt much of the story is influenced by real events and experiences. 'Next Stop Romance' manages to bring us along on a tale of kidnapping and romance all set during a time of bloody conflict, in a writing style that is entertaining and unique.

Born in 1891 to a nationalist family and no doubt influenced by his Fenian father and older brother Cahal Bradley (a distinguished politician, poet, and novelist), Hugh attended his first Sinn Fein meeting sometime around 1905 as a sixteen-year-old. From that first meeting until his emigration to New York in 1926 Hugh dedicated much of his life to the cause of Irish freedom. I could list for you some of his exploits and accomplishments from those times, but I think it's best if you read Hugh's own words. The following is from a letter he wrote in 1950 to the government in Dublin requesting a service medal:

> ...I joined the movement (Sinn Fein) when (Bulmer) Hobson first inaugurated it in Belfast... I remember we held meetings in an office building in Royal Avenue. Eoin MacNeil became leader. There were no designations as to rank. Those of us who were the pioneers of the movement especially in the North acted very much on our own initiative. I organized the volunteers in North Belfast, Ardoyne, and Marrowbone, and for a time was leader there, also I succeeded in transforming U.I.L in those areas into Young Ireland Movements.
>
> Our greatest problem was equipment, and I became a clerk in the British Ordnance in order to facilitate this important item. Along with Boland, Fitzgerald, DeValera, Carolon and

others I helped organize the Volunteers in Tyrone, Down and Armagh. And when Young Irelanders were few and far between, I acted as Volunteer escort to Markieicz, Cahoon, DeValera and others in Northern Ireland.

Throughout the struggle we had many changes in rank, even after G.H.Q. ceased being a floating entity. For instance, O'Duffy came to Belfast but left in a very short time.

One should bear in mind the part of Ireland in which we pioneers struggled for freedom is not yet free. The whole story is yet to be written.

I think I met you in Ballykinlar and it is a pleasure for me to know that a man of your ability is still serving our beloved Erin. I hope the time is not too far off when some of the glories of ancient Erin will be resurrected in a new Parliament preferably on Tara's Hill with every county represented by true Irishmen.

Sincerely Yours,

Hugh Bradley

Hugh was awarded his service medal. In his letter Hugh mentions that he may have met the recipient of his letter, an administrator for the government in Dublin, while they both imprisoned in the Ballykinlar Interment Camp. Hugh does not mention that he was arrested in December of 1920 for the shooting and wounding of a Special Constabulary officer on the corner of Butler Street and the Crumlin Road in Ardoyne. Shortly thereafter he was imprisoned at Ballykinlar from December of 1920 until December of 1921 when the peace treaty was finally signed. While in Ballykinlar Hugh was wounded when he was severely beaten with a rifle butt by a British soldier during the 'strike', a protest by the internees after two prisoners were gunned down in cold blood by a guard. The injury was so severe Hugh needed to be hospitalized. He stated in his pension request document that as a result of his injuries received in Ballykinlar he had suffered a 'nervous breakdown' and was having a difficult time finding work. In all probability he was suffering from PTSD.

Hugh was released from Ballykinlar after the peace treaty was signed but he did not return home to a peaceful Ireland. Civil war raged in the South and riots and killing between Catholics and Protestants continued in the North.

What Hugh did with his life between the time of his release and when he emigrated to New York in March of 1926 isa mystery, but we do know he returned to his family's home at 20 Herbert Street in Ardoyne and more than likely helped his father with his grocery business until his departure for America.

When Hugh finally left Ireland, one should keep in mind that he was not like a soldier leaving a foreign battlefield, he was leaving his home, the home he had dedicated so much of his life to, a home he had fought so long to free. A place he loved, bursting with the people and places he loved. The place where he played as a child and went to school, where he met and courted his wife Charlotte and the place where his son Charles was born in 1919.

When Hugh left Ireland he settled in Queens, New York and like most emigrants to America eventually came to love his adopted country, so much so he became a citizen, he even wrote songs about the city he now lived in. America was the country where his daughter was born, the country where his children went to school and grew up in and, the country his son would fight for during World War II.

Hugh did return to Belfast. He and his wife went over for an extended visit in 1938. They brought my mother along. She was ten years old at the time and one of the highlights of her life seeing Ireland and places where her parents lived and grew up.

My Grandfather died in 1962 and has been dead now for sixty years.

As I write this, I am weeks away from going to Ireland and I will be walking those same streets

Hugh walked so long ago for the first time in my life, with cousins I have never met. I think my Granda will be smiling down upon me as I walk into Holy Cross Church for the first time in my life accompanied by his brother's grandson Conor, who makes his home in Hugh's beloved Ardoyne.

- *Michael McDermott*

XIII

CHAPTER 1

I t's the month of November in the year 1905. The night is crisp, with the moon high, bright and full, when a youth pursues his way homeward – walking briskly around the "Horseshoe." He seems to be nonchalant in his gait, while at the same time the quickness of his movement, and his slender, neat outline on the roadway give to one the impression that here is indeed a precocious athlete. For a moment he hesitates, then stops and gazes upwards at the beautiful moon overhead. He glances to the right at Divis and then to left at Cave and Squires - the mountains and hills that are his favorite playgrounds. Turning around he looks longingly away in the distance towards Lough Neagh, the lake he had seen earlier in the evening from a nearer view. For what reason he ceased his hurried trend in the direction of the city of Belfast, in order to behold his surroundings, is difficult to guess; other than that, it was an inherent characteristic of his nature to dwell upon the beautiful, especially those scenes which present themselves at a psychological moment and require a transference from the physical to the mental effort, in order to study and perceive their great perfections.

A solitary country cart going in the direction of Crumlin attracted his attention. He stepped to the side and continued on his way, moving downwards toward the lighted city, that lay snugly in the deep valley below. He had almost reached Ligoniel, when to his right he noticed a signboard over a gateway, the entrance from which led to a powder magazine, which was built in close to the stone quarry. Moving nearer in order to read the words he was startled to see, "Danger, Dogs shot, Trespassers prosecuted". This is something new, he thought, because only yesterday he had lolled about the old quarries, along with his dog, Finn and nobody interfered. In the moonlight he could see that the magazine had been painted a bright red, and strong new locks were now on it.

He moved out onto the middle of the road and proceeded at a brisk pace, but as he did so he could not help thinking, "Why all these precautions; who, in the name of goodness would want to steal dynamite?"

Ligoniel was bright. Its lamps had been lighted and as Art slackened his pace and left the road, to walk along the footpath, one could see for the first time the features of this youth who moved over hill and dale, serenely – almost imperturbably, until the reading of that sign had set him wondering. His whole facial expression was so perfect that had it not been for the strong outline of his chin, and the rather deep masculine gaze of his countenance, a classification of effeminate would have been in order. Almost too good-looking for a boy. About five feet nine inches in height, broad shouldered with bright blue eyes and auburn hair would briefly be descriptive of his appearance at this moment.

He had left the footpath and its lights and was walking beneath the trees on the road to Ardoyne when he began thinking of the meeting that was to be held that night in the old hall. I wonder, he thought, what da's lecture is going to be on? I better move faster if I want to get there in time. Walking quicker, almost in a trot, he paused and raised his cap as he passed that beautiful edifice, Holy Cross Church, situated high up on the Crumlin Road. Having no watch, he guessed the time. It's eight o'clock almost, he thought. In less than a minute he had reached his house in Herbert Street. Finn jumped up to greet him and as he entered the parlor, the clock struck the hour.

CHAPTER 2

It was 8:15 P.M. when the Rev. Chairman, addressing those assembled in the old hall said, "There is no necessity in introducing the lecturer to you. He is well-known - in fact, he is one of the men who helped to build our first church for us when the order settled in this district – that was way back in 1868 - and strange as it may seem, the hall we are now in was once that same church. He is a man who has travelled far and seen much. Tonight, we are going to hear from him on a subject, in which he is well equipped to speak – "The American Flag."

Shamus O'Neill, Art's father, arose from his chair at the table and moved forward on the platform. For a man in his early seventies, he looked much younger. His forehead and the outline of his features bespoke intellect and determination, while his full graying hair harmonized with the deep gray eyes that swept across his audience here, he spoke the immortal words of Patrick Henry. "Give me liberty or give me death!"

When the applause which greeted him subsided, he began with a practical explanation of the construction of America's great flag, showing where the development and growth of the United States symbolized itself in the flag of that nation by way of additional stars. Speaking with emphasis, he drew an analogy between America and Ireland. "History has proven the righteousness of the cause for which Washington and his contemporaries fought the revolution with success, but how regrettable it is that a cause as just as that of the freedom of Ireland has yet to be attained." After pursuing his topic relentlessly and drawing to a close of what was a brilliant lecture, it was noticeable that he was speaking in tones filled with pathos, when he advised the large gathering of people that in their search for freedom, they would surely find it where the Stars and Stripes flew. Americans loved their flag because it was representative of that which really did exist. "Freedom and equal rights for all," he said.

Close to the exit at the rear of the hall stood Art. He was in company with two youths with whom he had grown up since childhood. In spite of the fact that he had little time for supper, he hurried and had succeeded in being able to arrive in time for the beginning of the lecture. His pals were enthusiastic and eager to discuss what had been said even before they had reached the outside. It seemed as though someone had raised a blind from a window and let the light into a room that was almost in total darkness. Jim Murphy, who was taller than Art, with dark hair and brown eyes looked amazedly around him as he reached the street and exclaimed, "Here we are living to this age and it's only now I realize that we aren't free."

Although they had roved the mountains and glens together and had seen nature in all her beauty as it existed in their beloved Erin, not for one moment had they discussed their status in their own country. Ernest O'Leary, who was about the same height as Art, with red hair and brown eyes and a disposition to be entirely fond of sports, said he had heard that a man named Bulmer Hobson had started a Young Ireland movement, the meetings of which were being held in Royal Avenue, Belfast and he suggested they join up. It was there and then agreed that the three youths should enlist in the new movement to free Ireland and they arranged to meet the next evening.

CHAPTER 3

Royal Avenue is the principal thoroughfare in Belfast. In an office building there, Bulmer Hobson had gathered around him about a dozen persons comprising young men and boys and amongst them were the three new members from Ardoyne. The leader (for that was what they called Hobson) seemed intent on having his followers concentrate their attention on the necessity of giving their earnest study to what he described as a new policy, called Sinn Fein. Like a teacher describing a subject to his class Bulmer delved into the pros and cons of the replica of Hungary's movement for independence. He laid stress on the words "Passive Resistance" as he reiterated the essentiality of absolute opposition to England.

This man who will undoubtedly rank as one of Ireland's greatest leaders, (that is in the respect of those qualities of education which it was necessary to impart in order to arouse a nonchalant manhood, to concern itself with the immediate problems of their country) was of that particular type which seems to require a closer and longer scrutiny, in order to access their characteristics.

Here was Hobson, a young man, teeming with ability, born and bred and brought up in the opposite camp to that of the majority of his fellow countrymen, a Protestant in religion who could have risen to a high position in the services of Britain, but whose love of and enthusiasm for his beloved Erin led him into this little office to form a "nucleus" from which he hoped would grow the force, that would eventually free his native land.

When those present relaxed from their studies, it was easy for them to form contact with one another and get properly acquainted. This led to free and easy discussion, and although it was admitted the task that lay ahead was formidable, their enthusiasm, plus their youthfulness gave to all a buoyant hope.

Toward the end of the meeting, the teacher (this is the name that should be given to Bulmer Hobson) would move among his class chatting with each individually. At such a physiological moment, one could very well form an estimate as to the appearance of this man whose knowledge was being imparted to his pupils. Of medium height, fresh complexion, high forehead and an expression that conveyed absolute sincerity, it was easy to discern that he was never meant for a situation that required force, being in entirety, an intellectual. There was no formal inauguration in so far as joining the organization was concerned at this time, and on their way back to their own district, Art, Jim and Ernest discussed the possibility of establishing a branch in their area.

CHAPTER 4

Time moved on and Sinn Fein Clubs were opened in three districts of Belfast, but the membership was so small that in Ardoyne, Art was able to accommodate the whole membership of his area in the rear attic of his home. Simultaneously, many branches had sprung up in Dublin and in various other places throughout the country. Arthur Griffiths, who formulated the policy which Bulmer Hobson was teaching so efficiently had been more successful in the south because he had a fertile ground at his disposal. The Ardoyne youths were ardent in their determination to preach the new "Gospel" and kept in touch with what they now called "Headquarters" in Royal Avenue. It was the last occasion in which they were to hear an address from the man they looked upon as their professor.

The office on this evening was packed full and it was noticeable that elderly persons as well as those of the opposite sex were beginning to join. Sinn Fein had now become the sanctuary wherein dwelt the movement that was eventually to fight for the freedom of Ireland. Namely, Oglish Na Eireann – Soldiers of Ireland.

The period between 1906 and 1913 was fraught with many historical events, in so far as constitutional agitation was concerned, but probably the most important could have been the successful political strategy of John Redmond in securing strong support in the English House of Commons for what he hoped would be the eventual passing of his Irish Home Rule Bill. Conflicting circumstances arose in Ireland at this time. Sinn Feiners had become more numerous and although they were a small minority, their arguments were being heard. The Home Rule measure was called by them a glorified county council bill. Even if passed, they claimed it would not give to the people control over finance or military and would leave the country under the supreme jurisdiction of Great Britain.

Although this was substantially true, strong opposition to it was developing among the Orangemen of the North and threats of revolt were being made openly from day to day. The youths who had formed the nucleus of the Young Ireland movement had grown up. They were no longer the pupils. Although small in numbers, most of them were efficient in those resources that were essential in the formation of a vital organization. They became closely allied with greater cohesion in all their enterprises and when changed circumstances required altered tactics, they were fully qualified to act upon their own initiative without an absolute dependency on directions from headquarters.

In later years this strategy served a useful purpose when as an army, orders emanating from G.H.Q. went amiss and never reached them.

Art had taken over the leadership in his district, but now that the organization was well established and the membership had grown, he thought it advisable to call for an election. He was duly elected leader, while Ernie became secretary and Jim who felt he had not the ability for a leading position, remained a member.

In the midst of the great tension that prevailed throughout the land, there were moments when some form of relaxation became necessary. It was Saint Patrick's night and the Annual Dance for the people of the district was being held in the old Ardoyne Hall. Art and his companions attended. They all found enjoyment in participating in the various dances and changed to new partners as often as the occasion required. Even when they moved in time with the music around the polished floor, it was noticeable that they spoke lowly but audibly, and at times as their conversations with their partners developed, soft smiles, even mild laughter ensued. For these same young men were naturally gay.

It was close to midnight when Jim entered through the front exit and walked across the floor. He had been to the bar to drown his shamrock. This was a practice indulged in by many on this festive occasion. It required one to swallow a leaf and wash it down with a drink. He looked rather grim for one who had been indulging and proceeded to the rear of the hall where Art was and sat down beside him. For a moment he didn't speak, wondering whether he should wait until the dance was over and not spoil their amusement on this happy occasion, but he decided it was his duty to tell the happenings – and at once.

The next dance, the Valeta, was announced. As the partners stepped out on the floor, he leaned forward and spoke to Art. "I have just come from the bar where I was told the police and military have raided your home. They have also made some arrests throughout the city."

"Keep calm," Art replied, "Go and tell Ernest what has happened and let's carry on as usual."

As the dance ended, a young lady left her partner and walked towards Art. She sat down beside him in the place that had just been vacated by Jim. Quietly she relaxed in her seat. The young man she was so close to paid little heed to this intrusion, other than that in a swift glance, he had seen someone very beautiful, and that person was now in close proximity to him. He had begun to consider the possibilities of a purely informal introduction, when the young lady broke the silence, and in a low voice said, "I beg your pardon, my name is Eileen O'Brien. I have a message for you. It's not too urgent and I'll give it to you if you'll meet me after the dance."

Realizing that, at a moment such as this, discretion was in order Art thanked her politely and watched as she arose and crossed the floor. Then he began thinking "Where did I hear that name before?"

It was customary for the Master of Ceremonies to call upon certain individuals to sing or otherwise entertain those present, and as Art had consented early in the night to give a character act, his name was now announced. Although it was nothing unusual for him to appear before a gathering in this capacity, he was for the first-time suffering from stage fright; for he now felt there was at least one in the audience who would notice the least defect. Moving forward to the footlights, he braced himself for his greatest effort and spoke deliberately as he said, "I am going to portray a very old Irishman reminiscing. The recitation is called 'Twenty-One'". As he sat in a chair with his legs crossed and a lighted pipe in his hand, he told the story with so much realism that the people assembled had focused their attention exclusively on him and watched him attentively as he pursued his vivid characterization. With him by way of contrast it was entirely different, because that reciprocal attachment which he was in the habit of giving to his subject while on the stage had faded, and at this early hour of the morning he was undoubtedly playing the entire part - for the dark, handsome young lady sitting near the front exit.

Bowing in acknowledgment to the applause that greeted him, he stepped quickly to the floor and walked directly to where Miss Eileen was seated. Speaking in a voice which to this suave young lady seemed rather flavored with familiarity he asked, "May I have the pleasure of this dance?" There was no answer, just a bow of acknowledgment and a faint smile.

It was the waltz and as they glided gracefully around the polished floor, in unison with the rhythm of the music, one could not help noticing that the dancing of the young lady was perfect, while that of her partner although fair, was amateurish.

The band had begun to play that familiar melody "We'll Not Go Home 'til Morning" when consternation broke loose in the hall. The military and police had broken in demanding that a complete search be made of the place. Shouting somewhat excitedly the master of ceremonies called upon those present to go to their seats and remain there until the authorities had carried out their duties. As Art accompanied his partner to her place, he asked quietly, "Where's the message?" "It's well hidden", she answered.

After a hurried search the Crown Forces left with nothing but the opprobrium of a people whose simple entertainment they had marred.

It was almost dawn when those who were present stood to attention and sang, "A Nation Once Again," Ireland's national anthem. After conversing with some friends, Art hastened to the cloak room where he donned an overcoat. The morning was chilly as he moved into the passageway leading to the door. There he stood waiting for someone whose first impression seemed now to be lasting. In a few minutes Miss Eileen, accompanied by another young lady, came along. She greeted him with the morning's salutation and as he stepped between them, said in a very formal way, "Mr. Art O'Neill, allow me to introduce you to my companion, Miss Alice

McLaughlin." Leaving the hall together, they walked down the road in the direction of the city. Their conversation was much like themselves, - gravitating toward drowsiness. When Art asked if they had far to go, Miss Eileen answered sleepily, "Just a few blocks." It wasn't long until they had reached the house. Miss Alice took a key from her bag, opened the door and after bidding Art, Good Morning - moved inside. Miss Eileen walked quickly in behind her, then hesitated for a moment, turned around and taking a letter from underneath her heavy coat, reached it to the young man who was following close behind. He bowed and thanked her, as she walked into the hallway awaiting as it were, a word from her that would give to him some hope of a renewal of their acquaintance, - but none was forthcoming. The door closed gently.

CHAPTER 5

In the British House of Commons, it looked as if the passage of the Home Rule Bill was inevitable. The Liberal Government under Prime Minister Asquith was in the position, with the aid of the Irish Nationalist vote to rally a majority. In the north of Ireland, the situation was tense. The Orangemen had already signed a covenant pledging themselves to fight against the enactment of any measure, setting up an Irish Parliament. Their leader, Sir Edward Carson arrived back from Germany, after visiting the Kaiser, and without any scruples, preached treason openly - threatening that the King's crown would be dumped in the Thames, if an all Ireland assembly were set up in Dublin. He called upon his followers for the formation of Ulster Volunteers and to show that his optimism, in courting rebellion was well-founded, a section of the British troops under General Gaugh in the Curragh Camp mutinied.

In the midst of all this the Government in Westminster

seemed to flounder. The Irish Leader, Redmond, who adhered to and depended upon constitutional procedure for all achievements in the political field, realizing the ineptitude of the English authorities, deputized that brilliant politician, Joseph Devlin from West Belfast to the task of enlisting the young men of the country in the National Volunteers. The call was as successful if not more so than that of Carson's to his followers. Soon thousands of men – on both sides of the fence - were drilling and learning the technique of war. Gun running became the order of the day. A ship sailed into Larne Harbour carrying arms for the Orange contingents and soon these quiet, unassuming men, who previous to Carson's outburst were silently attending to their own business, had now become troops marching openly on the streets - and armed to the teeth.

In the meantime, the Nationalists were making preparations to act in a some-what similar manner. It was not long until they too had thousands of rifles and bayonets and under the command of an ex-British colonel named Moore were playing war games and maneuvering on Divis Mountain.

Sinn Feiners with their Young Ireland movement were overwhelmed by this rush of the manhood of the country to enlist in the National Volunteers. It looked as if Civil War was imminent and there was no time for futile discussion. Action was now the order of the day.

Art, who had misgiving as to the whole trend of events, got in touch with his compatriots. They called a hurried conference and decided that maybe after all their place in this emergency was with the majority. It was so decreed that each individual would have the option of deciding whether or not he should join the National Volunteers. However, their leader told them that no matter what the future held in store, they must never forget that they were the pioneers of the movement that was fighting for the independence of their country and to act accordingly. The majority fell in line with the rest of their fellow countrymen.

The Ardoyne Contingent, which was attached to the Belfast Brigade, had two officers who were elected by vote. Art received a majority, and now was in a position to play a leading role in that army which he hoped would eventually free his native land. It was midnight and the Commandant had dropped into the Armory, (which was situated in the Falls district of Belfast), for inspection. Art, who was in charge of the guard, was seated by the fire smoking a cigarette. Shaun Mooney, for that was the name of the Commandant, had served with the British in India and was an expert in Military affairs. He began examining the rifles, the bulk of which were old Mausers. Looking down the barrels of some and surveying the others, he exclaimed "Where in heavens did these come from? They are gas pipes!"

The quality of the arms and ammunition distributed among the Nationalists was indeed of a very inferior grade - almost useless as weapons for war; but on the other hand, the equipment of the Orange Volunteers was modern and up to date. Their rifles, Lee Enfield's, were new - and stamped on the butts of them were the words "For God and Ulster. The Young Irelands learned this fact later on, when they captured an Orange Armory.

While the National Volunteers were guarding their equipment in one part of the city, the Ulster Volunteers, (for this was the name given to the men organized by Sir Edward Carson) were doing likewise. The youths who some time ago were raw recruits, playing at the game of war, had developed into two potential armies, awaiting the signal to spring at each other's throats. The Sinn Fein leaders suspected intrigue in high circles and warned their fellow countrymen of the danger that lay ahead.

CHAPTER 6

On the morning of the 4th of August 1914, the people were startled by a news flash to the effect that the Germans had invaded Belgium. The British cabinet lost no time, after a formal meeting in making a declaration of war on Germany. Consternation swept Ireland - particularly the Northern counties. Sir Edward Carson, the leader of the Ulster Volunteers called upon those whom he had equipped and armed for battle, to fight for King and country.

John Redmond, who was the Irish leader, hesitated awaiting the outcome of the Home Rule Bill, and after receiving a promise that the measure would be enacted at the end of hostilities, he sent the following terse message to his "Army" in Ireland: "Fight for Catholic Belgium!" A split ensued in the ranks of the National Volunteers. The small band of Sinn Feiners and Young Irelanders who had joined up with the majority of their fellow countrymen in the belief that civil war was inevitable, refused to accept the British government's assurance in respect to Home Rule - and resigned. Comparatively they were few in number and the great majority of the National Volunteers went overseas to fight for the freedom of small nations.

Art and his compatriots were right back to where they started from, but having been taught the rudiments of war, their respect for passive resistance was weakening. This new mentality that had developed in them was significant as a general trend, in other parts of the country. The war in Europe was raging. Ireland so far remained peaceful and calm and the men who remained at home to carry on the struggle for freedom had an interval of relaxation.

CHAPTER 7

It was late in the afternoon and Art who had spent the morning climbing the slopes of the Mourne Mountains to reach Slieve Donard, rested comfortably in a chair on the lounge of a hotel in Newcastle, Co. Down. He had a rude awakening when a young lady walked over to him and in a manner that was purely informal said, "You are Mr. Art O'Neill." "Yes!" he answered and looked up in surprise. "I came here especially on the recommendation of Miss Delaney, the teacher," she continued, "to ask if you would assist at the concert tonight by way of a character act or recitation. The proceeds will go to charity."

The young lady spoke these words in so expressive a manner that Art's attention became focused right away. Speaking with almost proud emphasis on the words, she said, "I am Elizabeth Barton". There came no immediate response from Art - he was still surveying her - even dreamily - but this did not in the least seen embarrassing to the one for whom he had nothing but eyes. She was used to being the center of attraction. "Yes," he at last answered. "I will be pleased to assist in any way." The striking resemblance of Miss Elizabeth to Miss Eileen was so complete that he could not help saying, "Please forgive my hesitancy, but your appearance has reflected the image of another, and I am somewhat confused." A slight giggle that was musical in effect greeted these remarks as she replied. "Oh! I know who you mean. Miss Eileen O'Brien - many people have spoken of us being much alike." Trying to be complimentary after she remarked that he looked tired, Art said," It is refreshing meeting you however." "Thanks, she replied, "I'll be expecting you." In a moment she had left him alone with his thoughts.

The memory of his first acquaintance with Miss Eileen was still with him. The impression made on him by her was lasting, and now that he had met Miss Elizabeth who was an actress, he was satisfied that the one he could not keep from continually thinking of, was indeed much akin to the young lady whose occupation was that of entertaining audiences. Now he remembered that he had once seen Miss Elizabeth play the part of the heroine in "Colleen Bawn". Turning in his chair to look through the window out at the sea, as if with aforethought in order to divert his mind, he still could not help thinking that all of Miss Eileen's beauty was duplicated in the person of the one he had just met. He watched the waves as they lashed the shore - each one as it were, making a mighty effort to go places, until by sheer exhaustion it surrendered to a period of retrogression and eased back to the place from whence it came, there to regain new vigor before renewing another onslaught. Realizing that the occasion required some little preparation, Art rose from his seat and went to his room and refreshed his mind by a small rehearsal. After a hastily prepared evening meal, he set out for the concert.

CHAPTER 8

It was a pleasant little gathering, purely a local turnout and no great effort to excel was required from an artist. Miss Elizabeth was at her best. This was a natural attribute so far as she was concerned, for even off the stage her demeanor was always at a high level. There was no dance afterwards and this gave to the people the opportunity to return to their homes early. Art and Miss Elizabeth had now become better acquainted. They sat chatting together in the dressing room and Art had now a chance to notice that although Miss Elizabeth's resemblance to that of Miss Eileen was almost complete - it was purely physical and ended there. He could very well see that she was in life, as in profession, an actress. Miss Eileen could never act. In fact it would be impossible for her, even for a moment - to be anyone other than herself. Most of the people had now left the hall and Art and Miss Elizabeth after a brief conversation with the officials, who thanked them ever so much, were soon on their way. It was a beautiful night and as both of them were staying in the same hotel, it was agreed that they walk back leisurely. She held Art's arm tightly as they stepped on the footpath 'neath the trees. There was an appealing tone in her voice when she asked if he would be prepared to join her in a charitable enterprise. It wasn't a favor, but something they both could conscientiously do and feel happy about afterwards. The young man on whom she almost leaned was deep in thought and hoped the request wouldn't be too great for his ability. "Anything within reason, Miss Elizabeth", he answered. Speaking perfectly, but quickly as they increased their pace, she told him that for a period, before becoming an actress, she had been a nurse in an Asylum and in that capacity had met the great Irish Entertainer, Patrick Wheatley, who was an inmate. Patrick told her that his wife, a London actress, had him certified as dangerous, during a drinking bout with the result he was locked up; while she, who was disloyal to him, took over possession of his assets and everything else that he held dear.

Certain members of the authorities were in league with Mrs. Wheatley, through outside friends. In fact, the whole thing was a pre-arranged plot - she told Art. Miss Elizabeth now went on to tell Art of some facts she had learned when working in the Asylum. The "higher ups" would take Patrick with them to social parties and have him entertain. These functions usually took place at night so they would return him the following morning. She insisted that the unfortunate man was perfectly sane and should be free. "I promised, if ever the opportunity availed itself - I would try and get him out," she concluded.

Art was overwhelmed by the plight of the man and felt that indeed something should be done. "What," he asked, "do you intend doing?" "Oh!" she replied, "I have all my plans ready - I only require your consent to help me." She held her tight hold on his arm awaiting a final answer. After a slight pause it came. "I'll assist you, Miss Elizabeth," was the reply.

They had now reached the hotel. It was getting late and time to retire. On the Mezzanine floor as they were about to part to go to their respective rooms, Art promised to be at her home in Belfast, early the next Thursday.

CHAPTER 9

When Art arrived at the door of the house in Glenhill Street, he looked at his watch, (he was growing with the times and now wore one). It was 9 o'clock. Being invited to have breakfast with Miss Elizabeth, he wished to be punctual. The beautiful young lady attended the bell and showed him into the drawing room, where the morning meal was being served. Everything around him was neat and orderly as he took his place at the table. He could now see that Miss Elizabeth had other accomplishments besides being an actress. Her gracefulness as she moved to and from the table and the rhythm of movement in her every act while serving – seemed to blend into perfect harmony of effort. It was only her great propensity to talk - too much, in a beautiful, cultured voice that had a marring effect. Once the conversation developed, she took control. As Art looked in her eyes and listened as she revealed her plans, he was attracted to her like a magnet. The thought that was uppermost in his mind, he even whispered to himself, "I could love her - only for Eileen."

It was now clear to him that the only feature that differentiated between Miss Eileen and Miss Elizabeth was the one that expressed itself in speech. The former he knew would never talk so long and loud, nor would she think it edifying to do so and he was certain she wouldn't ask him to do the things that the latter had planned for him to do now. These were some of the thoughts that filled his mind as he listened carefully and watched his table manners.

Miss Elizabeth now modulated her voice and spoke instructively as she told Art to go to the garage and bring the car to the front door. She said that as the morning was damp, she would wear oil skins and sit low down in the car - out of view. "You'll drive, Art", she said "and I'll give you further instructions on the way out to the institution."

Art rose from the table. As he moved toward the door there was a faint smile across his face. He was thinking of the words he had read in a poem at school when very young, "There's not to reason why." It would seem he had reached a stage in the situation that was developing where resistance was futile. In the garage everything was in readiness. Art made a quick test driving slowly and was satisfied everything was in tip-top condition. Leaving the car at the door, which he found half open, he walked into the hallway. Donned in oil skins, standing there awaiting him, was Miss Elizabeth. She told him to go up to the front room and change into the attire that was there. He obeyed even reluctantly and was back again in a few minutes dressed more stylishly than he ever had expected to be in his whole life. She looked at him admiringly and inwardly was satisfied that he suited the part he was about to play. Standing in front of the mirror, Art beheld himself in his new outfit: morning suit, raglan coat, butterfly collar with pale blue tie, spats, glossy shoes and gray bowler hat. All fitted perfectly.

Without delay they entered the car, she carried a parcel and moved close beside him on the driver's seat. As the car moved away, she gradually slid down until she was entirely out of view. From this position she gave her instructions as the car left the city and speed on its way out into the country. Art, on arrival at the asylum, was to ask for the matron. He was to tell her that he was over from London and had been appearing in vaudeville in Belfast and was now on his way back to England via Dublin and Holyhead. (This route she stressed with emphasis foreseeing the possibility of a chase and having her plans prepared to take them in another direction). Then he was to tell her he would like very much to see Mr. Patrick Wheatly as he had a message for him from his wife. In fact Mrs. Wheatly, on account of the air raids, was thinking of coming to Ireland and taking her husband out. On leaving he was to ask permission for Mr. Wheatly to accompany him to the gap as he wished to speak confidentially to him.

Miss Elizabeth said she would drive the car from the front gate and await then there. If all were clear and Art saw the possibility of moving out to the roadway, they could enter the car and be off. At the end of these instructions Art eased up, lit a cigar in order to have a "breather before the next act, in this drama of life in which he now found himself a participant, without the slightest premeditation. It was late in Autumn and the trees had shed their leaves. The two occupants in the car viewed the surroundings. Miss Elizabeth taking in the terrain, studying the possibilities of a get-away. Art didn't as yet give such a matter one thought. He gazed out upon the landscape and could not help thinking it was fortunate we humans had cracked the secret nucleus of the future by past experiences, else one would be inclined to bow in awe to what seemed now inevitable the end - but Spring would come again - and with it the resurrection. Miss Elizabeth said it was time to go. He stepped on the gas and the car sped on its way.

In less than a minute they had reached their destination. Hurriedly she gave Art a bundle of newspapers and magazines (all London Publications) and a box of cigars. For a moment she seemed to hesitate, as if in deep thought and then handed him a letter. This she said he was to give to Mr. Wheatly in the presence of the matron saying it was from May Deplez, which was the stage name of Mrs. Wheatly. Art looked at the handwriting on the envelope - then at her and asked, "Who wrote it?" "Never mind," she replied and with a smile she gave the command, "Get going!" He stepped from the car and strode up the pathway leading to the entrance. She looked after him with rising confidence.

CHAPTER 10

On entering the institution, Art began carrying out his instructions to their best possible advantage. He asked for the matron, and after relating everything to her in the manner that he had been "coached", asked to see Mr. Patrick Wheatly. There was very little delay. The old gentleman, who was beloved by everyone in the world of entertainment and now an inmate was brought in. Art who could be versatile at times greeted the great artist in the best theatrical manner. He reached him the papers and cigars, paused a moment and then handed him the letter saying it was from May Deplez - his wife - and for him to read it at his leisure later on. At this point the matron who seemed greatly interested in the conversation asked Art would he stay for dinner but an excuse by him that he had to catch the Dublin train, as he was travelling via Holyhead, was gracefully accepted by her. Art now began talking faster and expressed the wish that Mr. Wheatly be allowed to accompany him to the gap. Receiving this permission, he immediately took leave of those present and walked along with Mr. Wheatly on the path leading to the exit.

It was at this moment that Art kept wondering if his newfound friend was playing a part - the same as himself. He thought if this were so, undoubtedly, he was quite sane for his acting was superb. Looking around, Art noticed that two wardens were following close behind. Realizing that at least this part of the plan was about to go amiss, he shook hands with Mr. Wheatly and waved a farewell to the two custodians who were some yards further back. With a bound he was through the gap and on the roadway. The car was waiting and he stepped in. Miss Elizabeth was at the wheel and as she drove away, he told her what had happened. The car stopped to allow them to change places, while Miss Elizabeth resumed her place of hiding low down. A disconsolate expression swept her face as Art asked "What's next?" but even in this moment of sad disappointment she retained her charming beauty, and answered wearily, "We'll try again some other time."

Driving into a quiet nook on the roadway, Art eased up the car. He had seen the man they were doing so much for; and he felt there was justification in their act. After one long look at the landscape, he said to Miss Elizabeth. "I remember you telling me the inmates walked along the roadway, in the evening accompanied by wardens." "Yes," she answered, "about 3 P.M." Art was looking down at her. She had a pathetic look on her face. He could not help thinking that here, indeed, is one young lady who would even look beautiful in grief. Speaking in a voice that to her sounded optimistic, he said "Let's wait and make another try."

CHAPTER 11

Now Art took over where Miss Elizabeth left off. He drove around highways and byways, killing time and telling his partner, his part of the plans. On the approach of the time for the inmates to come out on the roadway, she was to leave the car and walk along the main pathway in the direction of the city. He would drive slowly through the crowd, and if necessary, sham a breakdown in order to ease up. As soon as he saw Mr. Wheatly, 'with the door ajar, he would move close to him, in some manner attract his attention and assist him into the car. If it so happened that the great artist was in the center of the crowd or walking in a position where the wardens' observation was clear there undoubtedly would be a chase - so it would be absolutely necessary to work fast. In such an emergency he would drive at full speed. He would not be able to pick her up and she would have to reach the city alone. If, on the other hand he was fortunate enough to "snatch" Mr. Wheatly without detection there would be time to stop and take her into the car as he sped in the direction of Belfast.

When he finished these words, he looked down at her and waited reactions. She was still hiding, and he could not help thinking of the beautiful garden flower he had once seen peeping from behind a broad green leaf. Miss Elizabeth, who was regaining her composure, spoke now in a reassuring way. "Very good Art," she almost shouted, "Carry on." Driving close to the curb on the byway, Art stopped. They got out and walked a short distance along a narrow pathway which was strewn with leaves. In the midst of their lonesome surroundings - the conversation became prolific. "I have something to tell you, Art", she said. "I was keeping it a secret until all was over, but you might as well know it now. I have legal advice on this important matter. It is," she continued, "if a lunatic escapes from an Asylum and remains free, without being captured for a period of two weeks, he can't be put back again unless he does something that would make it absolutely necessary. In other words, if Mr. Wheatly could be taken without due notice and hidden away for that period, he would then be a free man."

Art listened attentively. He had not for one moment ever thought of such a possibility and was glad to hear this. He resolved to bring this good man back into the world that loved him so much.

It was time to get into the car and ready for action once more. Soon they were back on the roadway which they had left. In the distance they could see the Institution, Art stopped and pointed the direction for Miss Elizabeth to go in. Silently the young lady left the car, smiled pleasantly and walked quietly the way she was told to go. Her partner, who was now sitting tightly at the wheel, moved on slowly. As he kept watch for any sign of the inmates, he soon saw in the distance a body of men. They were walking in his direction. Swinging the car around he drove right back for he had hurriedly decided that the best place to make his "bid" was after they had passed the highway. Speeding for a short distance, he eased up, got out and waited. Realizing that the critical stage in his plans was at hand he got back in the car, turned around and drove along the road toward the people who were now advancing on him. He was about to sound his horn, but on second thought, decided it would be better not to. The men were not marching in very good order and the guards who were in front and along the side, didn't look very much alert. Art now split through the crowd in an unorthodox manner with the car, at the same time being careful not to hurt anyone. He kept his eyes searching for Mr. Wheatly, and sure enough he spied him at the end of the crowd - walking alone. Leaving the door ajar - he leaned out, nodded and in a flash had caught the attention of the great artist, who with one bound - dashed in beside him. Driving like fury, he soon was clear of the road. Before turning on the highway, he looked back, but no one seemed to have taken the slightest notice of what had happened. There was very little traffic, and this allowed Art the opportunity to speed along at will. Soon he had overtaken Miss Elizabeth and in no time, she was in the car - greeting her long lost friend. Even in these precarious circumstances, this meeting was almost convivial. Switching clothes, that is, as much as possible, Mr. Wheatly was soon attired in the raglan overcoat, Bowler hat, collar and bow, while Art "donned" the regulation uniform of the Asylum. It looked much the same on him as a suit of "Dungarees" and attracted little or no attention.

The man who had just been snatched from a miserable existence, lit up a "havana", leaned back on his seat and looked once more like the great artist he once was. A "star" his profession. The car which the dexterous young driver had kept at a fast pace, soon reached the outskirts of the city. The occupants kept a sharp lookout for any sign that the authorities were on their track. Easing the pace, Art drove slowly into the traffic. An uneventful ride - without further incident brought them to the front of the house in Glenhill Street.

Mr. Wheatly and Miss Elizabeth got off the car and went inside immediately while Art drove to the garage. After discarding the number plate and returning the correct one to its place on the rear, he hastened back to find that dinner was being prepared. Hurriedly he went upstairs to the room in which he had changed his clothes earlier in the day, in order to take off his "dungarees". Here he found Mr. Wheatly who had just finished having a bath, dressing in new clothes, all of which were in readiness for him. Art quickly put on his own suit and went downstairs into the parluor. As they moved into their respective places at the table - one could not help noticing that although the occasion was fraught with the possibility of grave consequences, the immediate containment of happiness which permeated those present, would in some way be a fair recompense. The Great Artist realizing that once again he was the center of attraction, lit up the conversation with brilliancy. Holding onto that unique talent which seemed to belong to him alone, he sparkled with conviviality. When the meal was over, Miss Elizabeth lost no time and began hustling. She took Art aside and told him a taxi would arrive soon to take them to Bangor (a seaside resort in Co. Down). "I have all arrangements made", she said. "Mr. Wheatly will stay there under the name of Mr. Murphy, a retired gentleman from U.S.A. You will, of course, remain along with him as his nephew. At the end of a fortnight, I will arrive and take over. Mr. Wheatly will then be a free man, in a position to resume his professional activities. As she revealed this next part of her plans to Art, they had moved close to the hallway. For a moment he could not help looking into the depths of her beautiful eyes in order, if possible, to fathom what lay in store for the future. Then he looked away as if perplexed and thought of the words. "I would follow you down to hell, beauty maddens the soul - like wine." Suddenly she threw her arms around him, her cheek touching his and, in a whisper, said, "I am Mr. Wheatly's niece, so you see we are cousins."

There was little delay as the driver announced his arrival. Art placed the bags in their places and soon the car with all its occupants was on its way. There was a quietness among those inside, and only the chauffeur's voice could be heard asking instructions. Each one sensed the necessity for being discreet. To talk "shop", or rather speak of the task they were engaged on, would be dangerous. The taxi man might eavesdrop. This understanding lead to a complete serenity of temperament on the part of all - and silence became the order of the day, or rather night, for darkness had fallen over the landscape.

CHAPTER 12

It was late when they reached their destination and Miss Elizabeth lost no time in having them shown to their room in the hotel. It was quite comfortable looking with a double bed. After inspecting it, Art looked hard at Mr. Wheatly knowing he was to be a close partner with him during the slumber state. But what's the use, he thought, it's all in the cause! The young lady who had arranged to have these new guests treated in the best possible manner, made a quick survey and seeing that all was in order, got ready to be on her way. She bade them, "good-night" and as if in a hurry, rushed back to the taxi that was waiting outside. As Art and Mr. Wheatly moved to a table, near the window where a light supper was being served, they could see her wave from the street. It was near time to "hit the hay" and the two stalwarts who were through so much during the day, were beginning to feel the effects of it. Before retiring, Art took it upon himself to act in the role of psychiatrist. He asked Mr. Wheatly some pointed questions, studied his replies and after satisfying himself that everything was in order, lay down quietly on the comfortable bed. His partner, who had been accustomed to regular routine, was much more drowsy than he was and was soon fast asleep. Art who had kept awake awaiting this eventuality, soon followed suit.

CHAPTER 13

Mr. Wheatly awoke first, the next morning, and noticing that his newfound pal was fast asleep, reached for his bible, which was on a small table close to the bed. He sat up and began reading it. Being a deeply religious man, he had made this part of his daily routine. When Art awoke, shortly afterwards, he greeted with the morning salutation, looked at his watch, and in a "jiffy" was out on the floor. His companion followed the example set, and both of them were soon attending to their essential ablutions. When they were dressed and ready the proprietor showed them to their private room. Undoubtedly Miss Elizabeth had seen to it that the reservation was perfect. Spacious with large table and lounge chairs, the room also accommodated a good-sized library and piano, an ideal place for rest and relaxation.

Breakfast was served and the morning papers brought in. Art gave them a married glance in order to see if there was anything in them about the escapade he had been through, but not one word was to be found in regard to it. Mr. Wheatly's buoyant spirits now began to assert themselves. With a modulated voice, he sang "The Old Dandy" one of his famous hits, and then danced some steps lightly and with so much ease, that Art could not help applauding gently, although he comprised the entire audience. The great artist now related to him some of his experiences in the "Variety" world, as he travelled far and near. How in the old days when touring Canada and U. S. A. it was necessary in some places to travel by stagecoach and that on one occasion, when appearing in Chicago, he had a dispute with the management over financial arrangements and refused to appear before the audience. He had just reached his dressing room, he said, when a gang of hoodlums seized him and beat him up, threatening to take his life if he refused to go out on the stage.

The time was beginning to pass quicker than they had anticipated. At night they would stroll quietly along the beach. Three days passed by before any news of Mr. Wheatly's escape appeared in the newspapers. The statement issued by the authorities at the asylum said that he had been reported missing on Friday morning. This strengthened the belief Art had already in his mind that no one had seen what really did occur. However, as this was all the information to be obtained in regard to the matter, he proceeded in his usual way to pass the hours away, while awaiting developments.

CHAPTER 14

At the end of a week's time, Miss Elizabeth arrived. It was about noon and as she entered, Mr. Wheatly was entertaining Art at the piano. The meeting called for a hurried conference and as the young lady had obtained much information in regard to the whole affair, Mr. Wheatly and his companion listened attentively. It would seem, she told them, that there was no report made of anyone missing until the morning following the escape. This, she said, was very important and, she hoped, true as Mr. Wheatly was in the habit of going out with certain officials to entertain, usually at night. It was quite possible that some of the people in charge knew this and didn't bother making any report.

Miss Elizabeth seemed eager to talk and tell them everything she knew. The police had searched the trains going to Dublin. This she had learned from a friend who was there. It would seem no one knew what had become of Mr. Wheatly, but according to reports there were suspicions going around that he had been kidnapped by some London gang. Everything was going as well as could be expected, under the circumstances, she assured them.

Art now invited his pal to take his place at the piano and with an increased audience, the man who undoubtedly now was the center of attraction started singing songs which he had made great hits. The young lady then made a request and an offer. She said she would be pleased to act as accompanist if he would sing a song called, "The Solid Man". The great artist bowed politely and took his place near the piano. As the words and gestures flowed in unison with the convivial notes that sounded in concert, Art could not help thinking that so far as theatrical effect was concerned, the couple now entertaining were a perfect combination.

It was nightfall when Miss Elizabeth left in order to catch the last train home. On parting she advised them to be careful until her next visit, when the waiting period would be up. The hours once again had sped by. The two men who not so long ago were unknown to one another, had now become close friends, finding pleasure in each other's company, although anxiously awaiting the time when they could pursue their avocations in a more vigorous manner. The next day found them following the routine laid down by Miss Elizabeth minutely. The time slipped by without any undue incident.

CHAPTER 15

At last, the two weeks waiting period was ended. Art got busy preparing for his departure while Mr. Wheatly kept thumping the piano, as if in celebration of the great occasion. Miss Elizabeth arrived about her usual time - close to noon. She had nothing but good tidings. After questioning Art as to the health of his "charge", she told him that she would now take over. The young man who had done so much to oblige her was glad to be soon on his way back to the city and his occupation as a teacher. He had taken a vacation in order to help in this charitable enterprise and was satisfied that he was justified in what he had done. It was with a feeling of elation he made his friend, Mr. Wheatly, "So long!" saying, "I hope the circumstances under which we meet next time will give us both more room for expansion".

Miss Elizabeth now called Art aside. She said all arrangements had been made for Mr. Wheatly to enter upon his professional activities. Elaborating on the future possibilities in Theatricals, she was beginning to speak forcibly, when Art looked at his watch. This was a signal to her, that it was time to catch his train. As his eyes met hers the thought was in his mind. That those "powers of attraction" within her were dangerously at work again - and it was time for him to be going.

CHAPTER 16

When Art arrived in Belfast, he found everything much as usual. Soon he was back at work - teaching, and although his experiences had somewhat upset that equilibrium which he kept on all occasions, he was not preparing himself for future conquests. He had met Miss Eileen at Mass on Sunday and they both had taken a long stroll out in the country. From this renewal of acquaintance, a great friendship that followed was eventually climaxed by an ardent love match. This young couple were now seen together at the dances and when Art climbed the slopes of Divis Mountain, Miss Eileen was by his side.

The great war was raging. It had reached a stage where the situation was becoming critical, so far as England was concerned. The Irish people were threatened with conscription. Already the contribution from the Emerald Isle in manpower to the British Army was out of all proportion to the population. Sinn Feiners argued that a further call on the manhood of the nation would be serious. It was reported that Sir Roger Casement was in Germany. This man had served in various capacities for England. In fact, he was at one time in the inner circle and because of what he knew in regard to the British Government's intriguing methods in dealing with his native land, he had become antagonistic, and joined with his fellow countrymen in their demands for freedom. He went to Germany to counteract Sir Edward. Carson's mission there defaming Ireland, but unfortunately for him, war broke out and he was marooned. In spite of the fact that Sir Edward Carson preached treason, openly defied the Authorities, and instigated mutiny in the British Army, no action was taken against him, but when a German submarine left Sir Roger Casement high and dry on the West coast of Ireland, he was arrested, tried and executed.

Sir Edward Carson's great argument was that the protestants of the North, being of Scotch decent, were a different race. Sir Roger Casement was one of them, and a true Irish Patriot, while Sir Edward Carson (whose real name was Carsoni) was an adventurer. The true facts in regard to this matter are: Historically the Irish invaded Scotland and Wales. Even today the ancient language is still spoken in some parts of these countries, and it is fundamentally the same as that spoken in the Irish speaking districts in Ireland. It would seem that those people who claim to be a different race and live in the North of Ireland are, in reality, black sheep who have returned to the fold.

CHAPTER 17

It was Thursday before Easter and Art, who had begun his vacation, was seated in the parlour of his home reading a letter he had just received from Miss Elizabeth, when Jim Murphy dropped in to see him. Although they were closely associated in almost all of their enterprises, the "kidnapping" of Mr. Wheatly was an absolute secret and ethically, Art had decided to keep it that way.

Making an excuse that he had something important to attend to, he was about to go to his room upstairs, when Jim stepped in front of him saying, "I have something very important to tell you. Orders have emanated from General Headquarters, and I bring them to you. "All volunteers, fully equipped must report in Dublin Easter Sunday." He spoke these words as he was told to do. All messages during this period were verbal. Art moved over to his chair and sat down. He was not too much surprised because he had already known that there was to be a parade on Easter Monday, but the words "fully equipped" set him thinking. Jim moved closer to him and added, "It is recommended that each man bring with him a week's supply of food, preferably in cans". Art immediately realized the impact of it all now. He told Jim to go and see Ernie O'Leary, and that both of them were to get in touch with the small number of volunteers in their area. Going to his room upstairs Art finished reading the letter, in which Miss Elizabeth told him that Mr. Wheatly was about to enter into his professional activities, and wished him to become his manager. With as much haste as possible, the young man who now for saw more important duties ahead replied, regretting his inability to be with them, and sending his best wishes. He knew great events were impending and there was not much time for anything other than preparation. The orders went out, and that small band of Young Irelanders, who were attached to the Irish Volunteers, got busy pre-paring to go to Dublin. It being impossible for them to carry any arms other than small ones, these were procured, rations were packed, and although fully dressed uniforms were not available, a partial make up was in readiness.

It was Saturday before Easter when Art, through that mysterious channel called the "line", which Jim attended to with great dexterity, received word from Eoin MacNeill, leader of the Volunteers, canceling the order. Without more ado Art and his followers, who some time previous had planned to play Gaelic football, decided to go with the team to which they belonged to Newry, Co. Down. So instead of being in Dublin on

Easter Monday, 1916, they found themselves engaged in a stiff football match, with opponents who succeeded in making it a tie, the score being six points each. The game was over. The Ardoyne players were about to board the train for Belfast, when a trusted member of the Young Ireland Movement,brought the message to them that there was a rebellion in the city of Dublin. Art called a hurried conference of the members of the team who were Volunteers, and it was decided, that instead of going home they move into the area where the fight was taking place.

The Battle of Easter Week will stand out in the Annals of History as probably one of the greatest feats of heroism ever recorded. A handful of brave Irishmen challenged the might of Great Britain and astounded the people of the world by their unselfish patriotism. The executions which followed, although carried out according to military tradition, were undoubtedly murders committed by the British Crown Forces. Here were men, uniformed and part of an Army, who had been captured, taken out and shot in cold blood. Maybe the most atrocious act of all was that of firing on the Red Cross – and with a vengeance, when James Connally, a wounded prisoner was taken from his bed in a hospital, placed in a chair, and shot by a firing squad.

CHAPTER 18

With the exception of one of Art's compatriots who was captured and later interned in Frongoch Camp, all of the others, five in number, succeeded in getting through the British lines. The rebellion was over. Many brave men died but the people of Ireland were awakened. For a period, all was quiet; the calm, as it were, before the storm. The British Government had granted what they called an amnesty and the men who were prisoners in the internment camps were being released. This was political strategy in so far as the authorities were concerned. A general election was in the making and it required diplomacy in regard to the creation of a proper atmosphere. The Sinn Fein organization now became a potent factor in the political arena. Accepting the challenge of putting the issue to the people of the country, they contested every seat in Ireland and succeeded in electing 73 of 101 members to Parliament. This time the representatives were to remain in Ireland. They established their own Irish assembly and unanimously selected, that man of destiny, Eamon DeValera, as their leader. The Great War was at an end. Those Irishmen, who were fortunate enough to survive and had left home to fight for the freedom of small nations, returned to find their own country still in bondage.

For a period, the world was at ease. The people of Ireland awaited action by the British Government, that is, insofar as fulfilling its pledge to enact the Home Rule Bill but not a move was made in this direction. Art and his followers noted with concern that the place they were living in was seething and conflict seemed inevitable. It was now the year 1920. No overtures had yet been made by England in regard to Irish freedom and the Belfast Program was in full swing. Simultaneously, with military and police attacks on Sinn Feiners, the Orange mobs were making a concerted drive on nationalists, chasing them out of employment in the Shipyards and other industries throughout the city. Many innocent people lost their lives.

The Young Irelanders now realized that passive resistance was useless under such circumstances and had recourse to force. They hastily organized throughout the city and went into action with great effectiveness. In almost every county the volunteers, though few in number, were striking in the same manner for the freedom of their country. Their heroic efforts and achievements had won for them the acclaim of the people. It was only in Belfast and parts of Antrim and Down, where sections of the population were hostile that they found the task of fighting the British forces difficult.

CHAPTER 19

The Ardoyne contingent of Ireland's Army, under the guidance of Art was now growing stronger. Its numbers had increased, and their equipment was superior to that of any other body of volunteers in the country. For this reason, it was decided to give aid, where necessary, to any other company requiring it. It was a beautiful Sunday morning, and as the people came out of Mass in Holy Cross Church, they would form in small groups discussing various topics. However, on this particular occasion the pervading one was: What is going to happen in Ireland? Art, Jim and Ernest filed past the congregation. They had slipped quietly through the crowd because all the men who belonged to Ireland's "little army" were now "on the run", and found it necessary to keep, as much as possible, aloof from the populace. There was an air of mystery about these soldiers, and they prided themselves in the fact that they never made a mistake. Ernest, who was a Protestant in religion, had to be careful that none of his co-religionists would see him attending a Catholic place of worship.

They had moved to a nook outside the Ladies Chapel and were trying to anticipate the day's happenings when quietly, almost undetected, Miss Eileen confronted them. She simply looked straight and didn't speak but stood serenely - awaiting their reactions. A white Panama hat covered her head. From underneath it her dark hair peeped out by way of contrast. A dress of black crepe de Chine - fitted neatly her agile figure and harmonized perfectly with the whole conservatism of her attitude, as her soft hazel eyes met theirs. Although Art had now acquired a habit of surveying his surroundings, he could not look elsewhere than at the beautiful young lady in front of him. Only one thought that can be expressed in one word filled his mind at this moment - Apparition! "It's strange" he whispered to himself.

"I never can anticipate her when I look - she's there." Jim and Ernest now sensed the propriety of evacuating their positions at this psychological moment. They made hasty excuses and bowed almost begrudgingly, as if envious of their leader's good fortune. Miss Eileen turned quickly around and walked along the pathway leading to the road. Art, who had awakened, as it were, from his dream, swing by her side - and listened attentively as she spoke. "I have a message for you. It is from my cousin, John, in Ballydoindreen," she said. "You remember, on the first occasion we met, I gave you a letter from him." On hearing this Art took his eyes off her and surveyed the surroundings - in order to see that all was well. He then took the letter from her, opened it, and read the enclosed message which was:

> "The Black and Tans have occupied a mansion on the outskirts of the town. They are wantonly killing people by firing guns from a vantage point into the streets. They have burned and looted homes. We have sufficient men, but require more equipment and, if possible, explosives. Try and help."

Art realized at once that there was no time to lose. He was accustomed to meeting Miss Eileen, who was his sweetheart by appointment, but recently that became impossible. Although they were in love, their meetings had a formality about them that was only understandable to those who knew the circumstances under which this court ship was being carried on. He was leading part of an Army - which was being pursued relentlessly by an enemy. His time was not his own - and Miss Eileen and he must wait - for how long, no one could tell. When they reached the gate, both looking longingly at one another, "I'll attend to this," he said, and then continued. prophetically,

"The situation is desperate. I am afraid we won't meet again for some time." Their hands clasped as if their thoughts were in accord. Art felt tempted to move closer and kiss her, but their eyes met and he realized this was unnecessary - the spiritual embrace being complete. Without more ado he was off and Miss Eileen on her way home.

CHAPTER 20

Art fully realized the importance of his mission and hurried to headquarters, which was snugly hidden in a labyrinth of streets in the district. On entering he found that Jim and Ernest were already there. A conference between them began. It was decided to inspect equipment and see what of it could be spared for their compatriots in Ballydoindreen. Everything was looked into minutely, and after satisfying themselves that they could help in this respect – the problem of finding explosives was studied. Ernest had just finished an explanation in regard to the necessity of dynamite in the particular type of warfare that was being carried on against the enemy in the agrarian areas, namely the destruction of barracks, when Art remembered the powder magazine located in an isolated spot on the Horseshoe Line. In a flash, he had made up his mind and now issued an order. Looking across the table, where they were seated, at Jim he said, "You'll go to the Quarries situated on the road to Crumlin early tomorrow morning. Watch the movements of the men in charge of the explosives there and report back as soon as possible." Jim, who was fully alive to the necessity for quick action, nodded acquiescence.

It was a quiet evening in Ardoyne. A most unusual thing at this time, for the bark of guns hardly ever ceased being heard around the parish. The three young men who carried the responsibility for the protection of the area, now moved out in order to inspect the pickets, who were continually on duty. It was seldom that they visited their homes, but as there was a "lull" in the battle, they parted and seized upon this opportunity of spending a little while with their loved ones.

CHAPTER 21

The next morning saw Jim attending to his duties on the Horseshoe Line. As a lookout, he was "sharp" and his versatility was a great help in obtaining valuable information. It was not long until he was acquainted with the routine followed by the men whom he was to keep under observation. Early in the evening he reported back to Art the following: Two men who lived in Ligoniel were in charge of the dynamite. They arrived on foot, about 6:30 a.m., opened the door, took out a supply, which they put in a large portmanteau - and proceeded into the Quarries. They had no escort but were both armed with revolvers.

Art felt now that there must be no procrastinating. He told Ernest to instruct Harry Fitzgerald to be at "Johnny's Box", a junction on the Crumlin Road, with his car at 6:00 a.m. sharp the next morning. Now Harry was seldom approached in these matters. He was a trusted volunteer and a Taxi man by occupation. His services were always at the disposal of his fellow countrymen, but it was only in a case of emergency that he was called on. Punctuality had become a habit with these Young Irelanders, and at 6:00 a.m., at the place designated, a car arrived simultaneously with three young men, who entered it silently and unnoticed. The driver, who knew his work and the route, stepped on the gas and they were off. It wasn't long until they had reached the quarries and Art then began giving instructions. He told Harry to keep moving for at least a half mile (this was for the purpose of bringing them around a bend on the road) so that they would not arouse any suspicion by stopping. The car was close to the half mile mark which Art had set, when Jim, who had familiarized himself, in every aspect necessary, with the surroundings, said, "I think it's time to swing around". In a "jiffy" Harry was driving in the direction of the city. At the bend on the road he eased up, this being the best vantage point for watching the approach of anyone. Art told them to see that their guns were in order and not to move until they were sure that the door of the magazine was open.

Jim's keen eyes had now spotted the two men on whom they were waiting in the distance. He was seated beside the driver and nudged him with his elbow. In a moment the car was moving slowly along the road. The men whom they kept under close watch were now at the gate, and after opening it, walked along the pathway, beneath the quarries. Art spoke quietly to his companions saying, "Remember the element of surprise!" The car stopped. Jim and Ernest were first out and slipped quickly along the hedgerow, one on either side while Art and Harry silently walked along the path. They watched and waited till the men had the magazine door opened. Springing out from nowhere, they confronted them with guns. The hardy quarrymen were going to be no soft touch and though facing imminent death, reached for their revolvers. This possibility, the young men had already foreseen and like a flash Jim and Ernest leaped from behind and grabbed their guns before lead started flying. Harry and Art now went to work filling the portmanteau with sticks of dynamite, detonators and cartridges. Without delay the four Volunteers dashed for their car and there being no further incident, got in and sped along until they had reached Ballysillan.

Here a turn was made, and after a quick drive on a hilly road, the Marrowbone area was reached. The load of explosives was safely stored in one of their "Armories". Haste being necessary, Art called for a short deliberation amongst his pals. It was there and then decided that these same four Volunteers would leave for Ballydoindreen the next morning.

CHAPTER 22

I t was 8 a.m. the following day when Harry drove his car to the Armory. Art and his two companions had everything in readiness. They had assembled the equipment, mostly small arms, and put it in bags and repacked the explosives. With alacrity, the four volunteers were soon in their seats. Their "luggage" was tucked in neatly beside them. Fully aware of the fact that their abode, at least for some time now, would be a floating bomb, they crossed their fingers and hoped it wouldn't explode, at least of its own volition, until there was a more useful purpose for it to serve. In case of attack by Crown Forces or Black and Tans, they solemnly pledged themselves to fight till the end. "No Surrender" was to be their motto - under these extenuating circumstances.

Harry soon set the car going and there was complete silence, until they had reached Royal Avenue, the main thoroughfare in the city of Belfast. Here Art, who had been keeping a sharp "lookout" from the window, saw

Miss Alice McLaughlin. He knew her as Miss Eileen's friend, and they had met at the dance previously. Having the feeling that he would like to ask how his sweetheart, Miss Eileen, was, he risked asking the driver to move over to the curb and stop. Calling from the window to attract the young lady's attention, she soon recognized Art and came over to speak to him. The meeting had to be "snappy" as she was on her way to business, while the young men inside the car were on duty bound. She greeted with the morning salutation and speaking hurriedly told them that Miss Eileen had gone on a vacation to Ballydoindreen. Throwing the early news- paper into the car, Miss Alice said she was sorry but would have to be going. Art thanked her and Harry drove them once more in among the traffic. As the car slowly wended its way through the city's center, Ernest searched the paper the young lady had given them to see if there was any news in it of the seizure of dynamite, but there was not one word. Art said he thought this was very strange, but Jim who was an expert in circumstances such as those referred to, gave it as his opinion that the quarry men, in order to cover up their "blunder" in not being prepared, didn't make any report of the occurrence. It was agreed by all that this was a possibility.

The journey they were on was long and dangerous, but Harry who was well accustomed to driving in every part of Ireland, gave confidence to his "charges". He had been chauffeur to some of the prominent leaders in earlier escapades and knew just how to behave under almost all circumstances. He, along with his companions, fully realized that their greatest menace could come from an encounter with the Military, but their minds were set, and hell itself would not deter them from this path of righteousness. They passed many places that to them were familiar and there were quite a number of stops they would have liked to make, in order to meet men acting in the same capacity as themselves, but their leader had decided that in spite of the destruction wrought by the Black and Tans around them, it was necessary to concentrate on this particular effort and so the car sped along as quickly as possible toward its destination.

CHAPTER 23

It was nightfall when Harry drove the car into a by-way close to Ballydoindreen. As they moved near a farmhouse, the white walls of which could be seen in the darkness, Art noticed the outline of a man coming towards them. The driver set the brakes and quietly announced "Headquarters" to the occupants. The strange young man greeted them in "Gaelic" and then speaking in English invited them inside. He told them that the car and its "luggage" would be attended to. As they entered the doorway, Art noticed that it led into a broad room, lit up by oil lamps. A turf fire burned brightly, and neatly piled around it were utensils, undoubtedly being used in preparation for the meal about to be served. Two young ladies were busily engaged in laying the table, while six young men occupied chairs. Everything was quiet and there was little or no conversation. Then, almost smartly, a tall, dark, strongly built man, stepped in of the door. Looking around he saw Art and rushed to greet him in his Native language. They clasped hands and chatted for some time in Irish. It was clearly discernable to all that these two leaders had met before. John O'Hara, for this was the name of the Ardoyne men's "host" on this occasion, was the local commandant. He was a man in his early twenties, about six feet tall with grey eyes and fresh complexion that gave to him the appearance of one in perfect health. His aquiline nose, high forehead and firm lips, were evidence of a good intellect with determination. He now took hold of Art's arm and they both walked across the floor and through a doorway into another room. Here they sat down in privacy. The local leader, who seemed enthusiastic, lost no time in explaining what he believed to be, the essential procedure to be adopted on this critical occasion. He then explained to Art the situation as it really existed at the moment. The Black and Tans, he said, had occupied a mansion at the north end of the town. It was a veritable fortress full of ammunition and supplies. On a lawn in front of the building, overlooking the streets, two machine guns were mounted and with these the "tans" were wantonly killing innocent people. Day and night they had been intermittently "peppering the homes with bullets. "There's only two things left for us to do" he said, "and they are to destroy the building and "root" the enemy out". Art, who had listened with great interest, now asked him what immediate action was necessary, and when he thought it would be advisable to strike. Without hesitation, he replied that preparations had been made for the attack and all that was required now was the distribution of equipment and the lodgment of the explosives. "A few of my men, who have had experience in quarrying," he said, "worked undercover last night making placements underneath the gate and in some parts of the wall that partly surrounds the mansion, for the dynamite. Close to midnight they will continue their work, this time inserting the explosives and laying the fuses. If the weather continues good and keeps dry, tomorrow night the detonation will go off at 10 p.m. This will be the signal for attack. Art and he now got up from their seats, walked into the kitchen and took their places at the table.

The dinner served was attributing the efficiency of the two young ladies, who quietly went about their duties in quite an orderly way. Little conversation ensued during the meal and when it was over the Ardoyne contingent, pretty well exhausted after their long drive, accepted informal introductions all around and then sat down wearily on a couch.

The leaders, who kept close together, were the only ones inclined to talk. Intermittent gunfire alerted some of those present and a "scout" entered saying that the machine gunners had fired into the town and killed two persons. He said everything was well in hand and that the volunteers were now answering the guns. O'Hara, the local leader rose and went out. He returned in a short time and assured those present that the "tans" would never venture out of their fortress. Then he advised his "guests" to retire for the night.

CHAPTER 24

A youthful Ballydoindreen Volunteer showed the Belfast men to their beds, which were neatly arranged in a room at the far end of the house. Art lingered on for a while with the local Commandant, discussing some items of importance, until a "scout" entered saying "All's well". He then made tracks to "hit the hay". As he approached his bed near the window, he could tell by the calm rhythm of the breathing around him that his pals were fast asleep. "It's strange" thought, "but when men are imbued with faith in the cause of righteousness, their conscience will cradle them to a peaceful sleep. He lay down quietly and in no time had joined the others in that "slumber state".

The shooting had ceased outside and the countryside around the house where these rebels rested, was quiet. A great calm prevailed as the hours slid by, but the storm was brewing. Art was dreaming. Once again, he was with Miss Eileen, the girl he loved more than anyone else in the world. Then he became confused.

"Was it she?" he asked himself. A dark, handsome girl on the top of Divis Mountain. The heather was in full bloom and as they ran together, the soft breeze rippled the dark, wavy hair of his beautiful companion in the sunshine. Strange as it may seem he could not fathom the identity of the young lady. For a moment he was sure that she was Miss Eileen but when she looked up and called on the sun's rays to embrace her, he could have sworn then that she was Miss Elizabeth. Her voice had told him so, and he felt Miss Eileen would never speak so invitingly. The situation he found himself in was perplexing. Together they ran across the mountain, then stopped, while he held her hands. Looking into her eyes, he was almost certain she was Miss Eileen. Then in a voice that was pleasant for him to hear, she said, "Art, isn't everything around us beautiful." He was sure now who she was as he rushed forward to embrace her.

The guns were barking. The men in the room were all awake. Not a word was spoken. They seemed to be awaiting an order. A "scout" entered and said, "It's only a loud noise. Go to sleep again. All's well." Art and his companions, who had been long accustomed to this kind of unsettled rest, put their heads back on their pillows and were soon fast asleep.

CHAPTER 25

I t was late in the morning when the Ardoyne men awoke. They were fully refreshed and felt ready for all eventualities. Breakfast was served in much the same way as the evening meal. There were present the same six volunteers - the two young ladies, and the local leader, with an occasional "scout" moving in and out.

The weather was fine and as Art and John O'Hara got together for their first conference of the day, they both looked optimistic. When the morning meal was over, the local boys filed out as they came in, one by one, until they had all faded away. The girls also made their exit and Art and his companions were now free to discuss future possibilities in their campaign with the local Commandant.

The Ardoyne leader now began giving some instructions to his men. He said that Jim and Ernest were to concentrate their attention on the machine gunners, while Harry and he would follow "suit" keeping them covered. He reiterated the necessity of "surprise" and suggested that they keep as close as possible to the explosion in order to burst in first. "Quick action, if successful, would" he said, "raise the morale of all the other volunteers." Satisfied that he had said enough on this subject because his companions knew their work, he became almost cheery as he directed his pals to attend to their equipment.

Following the example set by the local men, the Ardoyne contingent filed out, and moved into the barn that was being used as an armory. The two leaders were now alone and remained for a while in deep thought. Art was thinking of the possibility of meeting Miss Eileen who was somewhere in the area but decided it would be indiscreet under the circumstances. All these men were practically "on the run" and seldom went near their own homes.

The local Commandant, who was related to Art's sweetheart, hadn't been in his own house for months. A long discussion between the two men lasted into the evening and only ended when a "scout" entered notifying them that the volunteers were filing in. John O'Hara nodded the messenger to assure him that it was all right and then said to Art, "It is fortunate that most of the people in the town will be attending a concert and dance tonight, which is going to be held quite a distance away. This, of course, will mean that the streets will be free of pedestrians in case of heavy firing".

Gradually the room filled up. Even the young ladies were in their respective places, doing their chores.

The organization seemed complete. Dinner was served earlier than the day before, but the same routine was followed and when the meal was over, everyone "faded away" into their respective places.

John O'Hara and Art rose from the table and sat down on the couch. Here they continued their deliberations. Now and then the guns would bark and some more innocent people die, but the local Commandant once more assured Art that the Black and Tans would not dare venture out of their armed fortress and were content to do these killings from a safe range. "We must go in and get them" he exclaimed, angerly!

CHAPTER 26

As darkness fell over the countryside, a quiet calm pervaded the men who were now assembling. The waiting hours had rapidly rolled by. It was 9:30 p.m. when the volunteers began moving out across the countryside to enter their positions. Art was surprised at the number of men mastered, but after consultation with John, learned that assistance had been sent in from other areas. The quarrymen, who were detailed off for the dynamiting, went out earlier and were now "dug in" at their posts. Three automobiles were outside waiting. One of these was to be used for carrying away casualties, while the other was to be stocked with seized ammunition. The third car belonged to the Ardoyne contingent. If all went well, it would be used to make the dash homeward with its occupants. Every man was now at his post. Slowly in the darkness, with lights out, the autos moved along the road leading to the rear gate of the mansion. When a safe distance was reached, the drivers eased up and the men got out. Harry swung his car around facing south, for that was his direction on leaving after the attack.

It was now 9:45 p.m. and there was a ominous silence. Those men who were assigned positions close to the gate were securely under cover. The local Commandant looked at his watch as best he could in the darkness and waited anxiously as the minutes ticked away. All around the whole countryside seemed sound asleep. Not even a noise from nearby farmyards disturbed the stillness. Ten O'clock sharp! A terrific explosion! The whole area shook with the vibration. Even the men close by found it necessary to mobilize their senses. With one bound the Ardoyne volunteers were through the opening - first, as instructed. The two sentries, whose boxes were close to the entrance, were completely knocked out. For some reasons the machine gunners still kept firing in the direction of the town, whether from force of habit, or distraction caused by what had happened - it was difficult to tell. Jim and Ernest lost no time and were soon on top of the nearest one. With their usual dexterity, they silenced him. Art and Harry were not so fortunate. They had some distance to go - and as they crossed in front of the building, a volley from the barricaded windows halted them in their strides. The former lost his hat but both of them were nearing their prey, and like a flash pounced upon it. The menace to the quiet folk of Ballydoindreen, from this quarter, was ended.

In the meantime, Jim and Ernest had swung the

captured gun around and now were "peppering' the barracks with a fusillade of bullets. Art and Harry followed this example and now the fight against those inside got going in deadly earnest. Volley after volley emitted from the apertures and windows of the mansion. The Tans inside had a good supply of ammunition and were now using it. A number of volunteers stormed the entrance and smashed down the doors but had to seek cover from grenades that were being flung out. Jim and Ernest, seeing this, moved the captured machine gun into a position covering the doors and cleared the hallway with a fusillade of bullets. The volunteers in the rear of the building had made progress and were closing in. Word had come through that they had broken into part of the building and that hand to hand fighting was in progress.

The local Commandant seized this opportunity to give the enemy and chance to surrender. He order a cease fire and called upon the garrison inside to surrender or die. The answer came in the form of a shower of bullets and grenades.

Art and Harry, who had eased up somewhat, now replied in deadly earnest. John O'Hara noticing that the resistance from inside had weakened, ordered another cease fire. Once again he called out for a surrender. This time an ominous silence followed. Then from out of a broken window, a rifle protruded, with a white handkerchief stuck on a bayonet. This was the signal that meant the end. Suddenly, out of the hallway came the garrison with their hands high up over their heads.

The volunteers, who had broken in at the rear, followed them closely.

No time was lost now. John O'Hara, the local Commandant, rushed over to Art told him that he and his men could be on their way. We'll blow up the building when the casualties and ammunition have been removed," he said. Both men shook hands but Art could not resist the temptation of wanting to know the price paid for such a great victory. "What are our losses?", he asked. "Two dead and three injured," John answered.

The Ardoyne men now left the scene of conflict and went to their car. They were about to enter it when a local volunteer called Art and reached him his hat. The leader from Belfast thanked him and said, "I think the wind blew it off." The young man smiled and then reached over and put his finger through the hole in the top of it. "It was very close", he said. The four Young Irelanders, who were now warriors, got into their automobile. Harry took over in his usual place at the wheel and in a "jiffy", they were off.

CHAPTER 27

S atisfied in their minds, that what remained to be cleaned up after this great achievement, was left in good hands, the men in the car relaxed in their seats. Harry drove slowly along the road. In the darkness he was finding it difficult to navigate but once the town was passed and the highway reached, the going got better. Speeding along freely, there being little or no traffic about, Ballydoindreen was now a good distance behind.

Driving around a curve on the roadway, Ferry was intent on leaving as much ground behind them as possible, but Jim who was forever alert, drew the attention of his pals to the sky in the distance, which was lighted up as if by a fire. Art, sensing danger ahead, ordered his men once again to prepare for all eventualities, saying "Our vigilance must be eternal". Harry slowed down the car and kept close to the curb in the hope of meeting some pedestrian from whom he could get some information. He was familiar with the area and after observing as best he could under the circumstances, said to Art, "I think it is the hell in which the concert and dance is being held that is burning". His leader now told him to drive faster and stop near the building – adding in a firm voice "Damn the consequences"!! The driver stepped on the gas. In less than a minute the car was in front of the hall which was on fire. With a keen lookout for any sign of attack, the men got out and moved among the crowd of people. Art asked an elderly man, who was standing half dazed, what had happened, but got no reply. He couldn't or wouldn't answer. It seemed that the terror in some instances had its effect. A woman nearby was different. She spoke up firmly when asked and said that the Black and Tans had broken into the hall during the dance and killed two young men and a girl from Belfast. "They then set the place a fire," she said. Art, who on all occasions was a man of steel, felt himself quivering for the first time, when he heard the words, "The girl from Belfast," a feeling of impending disaster swept over him. He knew Miss Eileen was vacationing somewhere in the area and even now, he felt her in close proximity to him. Only last night he had dreamed of her. Walking closer to the lawn, where a crowd of boys and girls were kneeling saying their Rosaries, he joined them. Looking down on the ground beside him he could see the bodies of the two youths. They had been dressed for the occasion and wore their dancing shoes.

He arose and looked in the direction of the hall. The fire had nearly burned itself out and the embers were cracking. All around was now in darkness. Art left this scene of tragedy and walked over to where another crowd of people were praying around the body of the dead girl. He looked down at the beautifully outlined figure, dressed in white, and stood in "awe". Bending over for a closer view, Art could see that the young lady had on her neat little feet, silver dancing shoes. He stood straight for a moment looking upwards, as if offering a silent prayer and then fell on his knees beside the body of the girl. Raising her head gently with his hands, his eyes swept the face that even in death, held fast to its beauty. "Eileen!!" he cried out, as he leaned over and kissed the cheek of the one he loved so well. A momentary weakness came over him but with a bound he was now on his feet and without realizing it, his hand was on his gun and vengeance in his eyes.

His pals, who were close by, had succeeded in gathering many important facts in regard to the occurrence and were prepared for the worst. A "scout" who was one of the local volunteers from Ballydoindreen arrived on the scene. He brought with him instructions from headquarters, for the Ardoyne men to be on their way immediately as the enemy was closing in on them. Harry went to the wheel of the car immediately and got ready for to go. Jim and Ernest brought the message to Art. They could see that he seemed dazed and was adamant in his determination to remain and fight alone. It was unusual for Jim to become soft but like the others, he could not help feeling upset at the tough break that had befallen his leader. "Art", he almost whispered "It's duty to be on our way." Falling on his knees with his head bowed, the young Ardoyne Commandant offered a silent prayer. For a moment he was alone with his thoughts. Then he felt a hand on his shoulder. Looking up he saw a priest standing over him. "My child, you must go. I will take care of her," a voice said to him. Art, who knew from past experiences that these men kept their word, rose to his feet and said, "Thank you, Father!" He then joined his companions and walked silently in the direction of the car.

CHAPTER 28

Harry was getting anxious when his compatriots arrived beside the car. The "scout" from Ballydoindreen, who had collected valuable information, had joined them and said that he was going to accompany them part of the way. They got into their seats and the driver sent the car spinning along.

A great sadness fell over them all as they left the scene of tragedy, but not one of them looked back. Ernest spoke first, trying to ease the tension by sending their thoughts in another direction. The weather is good", he said "and the road seems in fine condition for driving." "'Yes," answered Harry, "We should be able to make good time providing we encounter no obstacles on our way."

The "scout" who wasn't going far, now asked to be let off at the crossroads. Before leaving, he told them that he had found out who had committed these murders. "I have the names of the two men who are guilty," he said, and then he read them aloud. They will pay for their crime as soon as possible." Art, who was very attentive raised himself up. Like a flash his hand was once again on his gun. This time he pulled it out and kissed it. Then he handed it to the volunteer from Ballydoindreen saying, "With this please!" A farewell - and the Ardoyne contingent were on their way as quickly as their competent driver could take them. The car kept speeding over hill and dale, while the young men inside, trusted in good fortune to do the rest. Harry, who had been accustomed to driving in almost every part of the area they were covering now, knew the "spots" as he called them, for to replenish in. He also was proficient in his knowledge of the "whereabouts" of friends. It was part of his strategy to steer clear of town and villages and particularly places occupied by the Crown Forces.

CHAPTER 29

The night wore on. For a while now the journey would be reasonably safe only requiring skill in driving. Jim took over the wheel and this gave Harry an opportunity to rest. Joining his pals who were dozing over, the young driver relaxed on his seat. It was not long until all of the occupants inside were mildly asleep.

It was almost dawn when Art, whose rest was much "lighter" than that of the others, awoke and roused his pals. He told Jim to take a left turn at the crossroads and stop. Harry took over and after a fast drive, eased up at a farmhouse, which was snugly situated below a hill surrounded by trees. Here they got out and went inside. In haste they freshened up with a kind of morning ablutions. Breakfast was served, during which the proprietor attended the replenishing necessary to the car. There was no delay. Conversations were "out" and their host who was a trusted patriot, understood and facilitated their efforts to move fast. As they entered their car for the last part of their journey homeward all but Art were fresh and vigorous. He was weighed down by grief.

Alertness was absolutely essential now as Harry gradually increased his speed on the way homeward. The going was smooth for the rest of the journey, it being the case that roads nearing the outskirts of the city are almost always kept in good condition. It was past noon when Harry drove the car into the suburbs of the city of Belfast. He then stopped. Art, Jim and Ernest got out. The three Volunteers walked away separately, as pre-arranged, to go to their district by different routes. Driving with caution, the young stalwart at the wheel, moved in among the traffic and soon was lost. He too was homeward bound, but unlike the others, lived in the center of enemy territory. On the edge of a volcano, as it were, and realizing this he was always "on his toes".

CHAPTER 30

A rt experienced great difficulty in reaching headquarters. It was late in the evening before he succeeded in getting through. Gunfire and sniping were prevalent all over the city and as he entered his area, the pickets told him that the fighting had been severe. He went into conference immediately with those men who had taken over during his absence. From them he learned that the general situation was precarious. They told him that on the night previous, fierce battles had taken place, and the streets were strewn with the dead and injured. One of the weak nationalist areas had caved in, they said under the onslaught. Jim and Ernest, who now had also been acquainted with the seriousness of the situation, arrived in haste. The former, speaking boldly, said that what was required was more men and guns. "Why", he said angrily "If the Volunteers weren't here to defend the people of this city, they would have been massacred, or driven out long ago." Art, without hesitation issued an order, calling upon all men in the area to protect the district. The response was good, and Ardoyne became a veritable fortress with no one being able to enter, or leave, without the strictest scrutiny. The other Nationalist parishes followed this example, and the Volunteers, who had now designated themselves the Irish Republican Army, became a formidable force.

When their duties were attended to, Art promised Jim and Ernest that they would be able to snatch a night's rest. They were about to leave, when the newsboy threw in the evening paper. Ernest took it and glanced quickly at the headlines. He noticed a late report and read it out aloud to his companions. It said, "The bodies of two Black and Tans were found on the roadway near Ballydoindreen today - labels were attached to each with the following words written on them, 'Executed by Irish Republican Army." Art took the paper from his pal and looked at the names which were printed below. "We never make a mistake," he said.

It was now arranged that Jim and Ernest would take over early the next morning while their leader would rest up until later in the day. The three young Irish Republican Army men now left headquarters together. There was a great silence after the storm and they decided to take a chance and go to their respective homes. On their way along the street the conversation had developed and Jim asked Art a pointed question. What is the reason," he asked, "the regular British troops only enter into conflict with us when we have the others beaten?" The Ardoyne Commandant who, as well as being a fighter, was a strategist in political expediency, answered, "The British Government, as you are aware Jim, prides itself in the efficiency of its Army, and wishes to keep it clean. The men in control in London, know that they are engaged in an unjust fight and there is dirty work to do, so they supplement their army with auxiliary forces, called Black and Tans, in the hope that with their disbandment, will go the memories of the atrocities committed. Here, you know, they are wrong for we Irish have long memories, and will never give up the struggle until our country is free." They had now reached Art's home and after bidding his pals good night in error for it was now morning – Art opened the door and entered the house quietly.

CHAPTER 31

It was a beautiful morning - with not one rifle shot to mar the peacefulness of it all. The men in headquarters felt relieved at even this small break and took it easy. Jim and Ernest were at their posts early and had not long taken over when the "line" arrived (By the way, this was the name given to the man who carried the dispatches). He delivered two messages and without more ado, went his way. After Jim had read the first one, he looked at Ernest and said in surprise, "A truce has been declared between the Irish Republican Army and the British Crown Forces!" For a moment the two companions who had been in this fight since its beginning, looked at each other. Neither of them spoke, but they both had the same line of thought. They were wondering what was going to happen next. The second message was now opened by the young man substituting for Art. It was from Ballydoindreen and said that the mansion had been blown up and all was quiet. Jim seemed to flounder as he read in a note attached, that the name of the young lady who had been murdered that night outside the hall, where the concert and dance was being held, was Miss Elizabeth Barton, an actress from Belfast. This news was a revelation to him and looking at Ernest, he shouted, "What a blunder we have made! Come here and read this!" When his "aide" finished reading the dispatch and note, he just didn't know what to say.

Both of them who realized that their leader was bowed down with grief over what he believed to be the loss of his beloved sweetheart, now began searching their minds for a way out. Ernest was the first to speak, "Jim", he said, "Art must receive this news in some appropriate manner. I have an idea," he continued, "Let me get in touch with Miss Eileen O'Brien as soon as possible. With this truce on, it will be safe to move around. She, as you will remember used to carry dispatches for us... I will ask her to bring these two to Art.

We will then have done our part. The rest will be up to him." Jim acquiesced, saying, "All right Ernest. You're an artist and know the essentials required in procedure for depicting a beautiful scene. "Get going!"

It was almost noon when Art, who had a late breakfast, got dressed and ready to go out. He had just put on his coat when there was a ring on the doorbell. His sister, who had attended to it, came back and told him a young lady wished to see him. He asked that she be shown into the parlour. It was customary for people to want to see him, but as this was the first occasion, in a long time, that he had been in his own house, the thought struck him of it being rather peculiar. However, he braced himself up for the occasion and without pursuing his thoughts further, went into the room where the young lady was waiting.

On entering, he was about to exclaim, "Miss Elizabeth, why did you risk coming here?" but the young lady had risen from her seat, and the sunbeams which streamed through the windows lit up her face. He looked straight at her, with eyes that the strenuous times he had been through, had almost made fierce. The soft look that responded from the dark, handsome, young lady now standing in front of him, sent a "quiver" of doubt through his mind. Then came the words, "I bring you these dispatches, Art" from lips that faintly smiled. The sound of the voice unlocked the young Commandant's mind of all its uncertainties, "Eileen!" he cried out "It's you!" Taking her in his arms he kissed her wildly. The decorum of the young lady was upset. Their meetings on all occasions were purely formal. When she had regained her equilibrium, the thought struck her that maybe he had heard of the truce and was elated.

It was never part of Art's routine to delay attending to dispatches, but the circumstances on this occasion had overwhelmed him. He quickly read the message from Ballydoindreen. "Gearing his mind for its highest effort, he resolved that Miss Eileen would never know the facts about this incident, at least for a long time. The dispatch telling of a truce was a pleasant surprise to him. The fierce look, acquired through peril and hardship, softened in him eyes, as he moved forward to embrace his beloved. Eileen! he said, "Have you heard the good news?" "Yes" she replied, "I'm delighted," then asked, "Art, do you think Ireland will ever be a free and united nation." The answer was swift and assuring. "Yes, darling, eventually our country will be a nation "one and indivisible" - like you and I."

They moved closer to the window and looked out into the sunshine. This time Art spoke, softly (just like her), "Will you marry me?" he asked. There was no hesitancy as the Beautiful loved one answered, firmly (just like him) "Yes!" As their lips met, so did their thoughts. "Art" she said, "Next to you, I loved Miss Elizabeth better than anyone else I ever met." These words reflected the sentiments of the young man to whom they were spoken so much, that he replied, "Yes, darling, I'll never forget her!!! and then he thought - "How could I, with Eileen for my wife?"

AFTERWORD

I can recall countless times as a young boy poking around in the bottom drawer of my mother's china cabinet. For years my grandfather Hugh Bradley's manuscript 'Next Stop Romance' sat in that drawer. The bottom drawer was where my mother put the items that were special to her. There were boxes of post cards and old photographs of places and people I didn't recognize. Her high school yearbook was in there along with various knickknacks she had collected over the years that would hold no value to anyone but her. I remember there were copies of Life magazine in the drawer, all dedicated to the presidency of John Fitzgerald Kennedy. Like all Irish American families JFK was a hero in our house. A framed photograph of Kennedy hung in the hallway of our home for years. 'An Irish Catholic in the White House', even I understood the significance of that because I knew at an early age, I was Irish. Other kids on the block were Italian Americans or Jewish Americans or German Americans or just plain Americans but we were Irish Americans, and it was important to my parents that we kids knew we were Irish. We seemed to be the only Irish kids in this sea of diversity we had moved into. We came from the Irish enclave of Woodside Queens. Woodside was an old Irish neighborhood. If you took out the New York City phone book and read out the names of the people who lived in Woodside, it would be a long time waiting before you ran across a name that wasn't Irish. This is where my parents were from, but now, we were the only Irish family on the block. But my parents continued to do what Irish people from Woodside did, so every Sunday after mass the Irish phonograph records would come out and the Irish music would fill the house. The Clancy Brothers would sing rebel songs and the great tenor John McCormack would croone the old Irish classics. On many of those Sundays, my Uncle Charlie would drive out from Queens to our house on Long Island and he would bring my Granda with him.

I had known my Granda since the day I was born. He would visit us in the apartment in Woodside. When we first left Woodside, I was an unhappy kid. I missed all the relatives who had fawned all over me. In addition to my Uncle Charlie and Granda, there were my father's family and tons of friends my parents had known forever. We all lived close by and we were always visiting each other, and all the woman seemed to marvel at what a 'big boy' or 'smart boy' or 'handsome boy' I was. Perhaps that's what saddened me the most about leaving Woodside, I missed all the attention I had received. I remember my mother pushing my brother

Tommy in the baby carriage down Roosevelt Avenue with me and my sister Margaret in tow. It seemed she knew everyone. People would stop to talk, mostly woman friends and of course they would comment on how adorable we all were. But that all ended for me when at the tender age of four we left good old Woodside for the suburbs of Long Island, where we knew no one.

Our new home, in a place called Wantagh, was so very different from the apartment we had lived in. We had a nice back yard with trees and the house was on a quiet street. There was no rattle every ten minutes from elevated subway trains like there was in the old apartment. The house had plenty of room for us kids. Four bedrooms, living room, dining room, kitchen, full basement where we could play in the bad weather. We were close to the beach. There were baseball fields and playgrounds. Parents could let their kids go out to play or ride bikes without the worry they might get run over by a car or hit by a bus. It was the 'American Dream' come true and my parents hated it. They missed the intimacy of Woodside. The Long Island suburbs were too planed and impersonal for them. My mom and dad loved walking down the crowded streets of Woodside to church or the stores and bumping into friends and chatting. They loved the organized chaos of Queens. My mom would always say we should have never left Woodside, and when us kids were all grown up, she said her and my dad were going to move back and get an apartment where they could walk to church and the stores and get a beer at Barry McLeary's Bar and take the subway into the city to see a Broadway show once in a while. But they never did move back. Both my parents died in that house in Wantagh.

As I said, I was about four when we moved, and it wasn't long before I too was wishing we were back in Woodside. I made friends with a kid my age around the corner from us. We were playing and for some reason I can't remember anymore, we had fight and I ended up coming home crying. That Sunday Granda was over the house. When he found out about the fight, he decided I needed a bit of training in the manly art of boxing. So, he took me downstairs to the basement and gave me a quick lesson. I was all of four and I can still remember him on his knees showing me how to hold my little fists up and how to throw a punch. He held his palms out while I hit them with jabs and hooks and uppercuts. The lesson was probably all of ten minutes and I really didn't learn much boxing, after all I was a just a little kid but my Granda saying 'ouch' when I hit his palms and telling me I had the makings of a great boxer someday gave a scared little four-year-old kid who was new in the neighborhood a bit of confidence.

I loved my Granda, and I know he loved us kids. He would always have time for us. He had a way making us feel like the occurrences in our little lives were very important and that we were indeed special kids. So, we would hear him encouraging us with compliments: "Go Tommy go, I don't think I've ever seen a boy ride a tricycle so fast in me entire life." "Margret dear, you must have the prettiest singing voice in the whole country." "Sure Michael, I think you throw that baseball faster than Whitey Ford when he was your age" (the great New York Yankee pitcher grew up across the street from the Bradley family).

In 1959 the Disney movie 'Darby O'Gill and the Little People' came out. Of course, my parents took me and my sister to see it. It was the first movie I recall seeing in a move theater and it had a lasting effect on me at the time. I had looked forward to seeing Darby O'Gill because I was told it had leprechauns in it. What kid wouldn't want to see a movie with leprechauns. But it also had a banshee and a death coach. I wasn't told about the banshee and the death coach, and these parts of the movie terrified me and gave me nightmares for days. I still remember lying awake too frightened to sleep worrying that I was going to get a visit from a banshee who would lock me in a death coach and take me away. My mom told me to stop fretting over banshees and death coaches because there was no such thing. But I was too cleaver to accept that as an answer. Afterall my mom was an American, like me. What would she know about it? But I knew I had a source who would know all about the subject of banshees and death coaches. My Granda of course. He was from Ireland. He had lived there. He even sounded like Darby O'Gill when he talked and without his glasses, he kind of looked a bit like him to me. I couldn't wait until his next visit so I could talk to my Granda about the subject.

When my Granda finally came over we had a conversation in the backyard about Darby O'Gill, leprechauns, banshees, and death coaches. I remember him sitting me up on a low branch of our little maple tree so we could talk face to face. He assured me that banshees and death coaches were not real, and I had nothing to worry about. He said that it was something that was made up in the old days to scare people, like ghost stories. I asked him about leprechauns and for some reason he told me leprechauns were indeed real. I was delighted hear this. Little men with gold running around the countryside. Ireland must be a wonderful place! Perhaps Granda regretted our conversation because it wasn't long afterwards that he announced he was going to take a trip back home to Ireland. This was great news to me because now Granda would be able to capture a leprechaun and bring it back to America for me along with any gold he might get out of the little fellow as well. I envisioned keeping a leprechaun as my captive and taking him out to entertain the kids in the neighborhood whenever it pleased me. I could even show him off to my class at school.

I couldn't wait for Granda to return from Ireland. I would have a real live leprechaun! I would be able to make wishes. I'd wish for a horse and a dog and to be able to fly like Superman. Granda must have known he had backed himself into a corner by telling me leprechauns were real. And I suppose he didn't want to disappoint me by just saying he couldn't catch one, so he bought me a souvenir leprechaun doll and concocted a tale about why my leprechaun, although now nothing more than a stuffed doll, was once a living breathing leprechaun. The story telling was done with great dramatic acting and went something like this:

My Granda was awakened by a leprechaun singing in the dead of night. Putting on his clothes my Granda took a big Shaefer beer stein from the kitchen. Shaefer Beer was a New York based beer company my Uncle Charlie did business with, so what a Shaefer beer stein was doing in a kitchen in Ireland went unexplained. Granda snuck out quietly into the woods where the unsuspecting little leprechaun was singing and dancing. He was so preoccupied that Granda was able to crawl slowly up behind the leprechaun and with great speed and dexterity was able to trap him under the beer stein.

Granda held the little fella captive the rest of his stay. When it was time to return to New York Granda kept the beer stein with the trapped leprechaun inside on his lap during the plane ride. All was well, but as the plane was taking off the little fella somehow escaped. Of course, with a leprechaun loose on the plane all kinds of confusion and chaos ensued until the plane reached the sea and was no longer over Ireland. What happened then was nothing short of amazing. The little fella who has been wreaking havoc suddenly turned from flesh and blood into the cloth and plastic doll that my Granda gave to me. He told me the transformation occurred because leprechauns can only live in Ireland and once the plane was no longer over Irish land 'poof' the little fella turned into the doll. He knew even at four years of age I may doubt the validity of such a tale, so he showed me the beer stein as proof that the whole story was indeed the truth. My disappointment must have been apparent so my mom helped a bit with the conspiracy by telling me afterwards that sometimes she would awaken at night to find Seamus, that was the name the doll was given, on her china cabinet dancing and singing the Irish tune 'Nell Flaherty's Drake'.

My Granda died in 1962. He was seventy-one years old, and I was seven. I remember the last visit he made to our house out on Long Island. I can still see my Uncle Charlie's car pulling into our driveway from across the street where I was playing with friends. I remember my Granda was slouched over in the passenger seat. We were told Granda was sick, but we didn't know he was dying. I guess my mom felt we were too young for that terrible news. He had come out to see us one last time, his daughter, and her children, five of us by that time. We were his only grandchildren.

When Uncle Charlie's car came to a stop my mom and dad came running out of the house to help Granda out of the car. "Granda," I called out as I ran across the street, but I was cut off along with my brother and sister by my mom. "You kids stay out here and play for a while. We'll call you in when your Granda is settled in. You know he's not feeling good. Now off you go." So, we waited around to be allowed in. Finally, my mother opened the front door, "All right you kids can come in now."

Granda was seated in a chair in the living room. My dad and Uncle Charlie were on the couch. I think a baseball game was on TV, but I couldn't swear to it. I went over to see Granda. He tried to be his old cheerful self, as he always had been around us kids, but he didn't have the energy. His face was drawn, his skin was a bit gray, and he was thin and the way he looked frightened me. To this day when I recall how I reacted when I saw him that last time, I feel horrible, and I wonder if he saw the fear in me when I looked at him that day.

After he died and as I grew older my mother would try to keep my grandfather's memory alive with stories of his past in Ireland, but they were vague and never had much detail. She told us he was in the old IRA in Belfast during the war with Brittan and the Orangemen and that he had been imprisoned. She told us he had been a teacher and that his brother had been a great politician and writer. She told us that Granda and her mother had taken her back to Ireland when she was a young girl to meet all his family and to see the old neighborhood and the house where he had lived, and that is was a wonderful place. But as the years went on these stories were told less and less and the Irish music that was played on the stereo was replaced by rock and roll and we kids became less Irish and more American. We would sometimes go into the city to watch the St. Patrick's Day Parade and of course like all Irish Americans we would watch the great John Wayne movie the 'Quiet Man' whenever it came on the TV, but not much more than that. After a while we didn't even go into Woodside anymore, the old people began to die off and the younger people moved their families out to Long Island. And we kids began to grow up.

During the troubles, Northern Ireland and Irish nationalism was at the forefront in the McDermott household for the first time in a long time. The evening news lead with stories of shooting and riots in Belfast and across all of Ulster. When a cousin joined the Hunger Strike in Long Kesh his mother reached out to my parents to see if we could help in any way. For the first time in their lives my parents become politically involved in an issue. A childhood friend of mine was on the staff of the U.S. Senator from New York. Through him my parents contacted the Senator who saw a political opportunity to help with a popular cause in the states. Letters were written to the White House from the Senator on our behalf asking President Reagan to put pressure on the British government to end the hunger strike, but Reagan was a great admirer of Margret Thatcher and did little in the way of helping the Catholic people of Northern Ireland. I am bit ashamed to say that while my parents were working on their campaign to help the hunger strikers I was not. I was busy living the life of a young man on Long Island;

going to bars, night clubs, the beach and ballgames and doing as little work as possible in between.

3 February 2021

Hello Michael,

My name is Conor Bradley, we are related. Hugh Bradley was my great uncle. His brother Charlie was my granda. I've just started my family tree and found your tree. I have found Charlie's manuscripts and published them. We'll have to share our finds.

Kind regards,

Conor

I received this email through Ancestry.com. I had subscribed to the genealogy website to research my family's history. Like many retirees, I found myself with time on my hands. I had seen commercials for Ancestry on TV, and I thought it would be fun to see if I could piece together my family's history. I wanted to find about my Granda Hugh and his family as well as my paternal grandfather, a World War I veteran, who I never met. So, I subscribed and began setting up a family tree. I found a bit of information. I was able to find out the names and ages of all of Hugh's siblings, where they lived, the names and ages of Hugh's parents, the 1926 immigration documents for Hugh and his wife Charlotte, where they lived in

Queens and a few more tidbits but not much more than that.

So, I connected with Conor, who had a passion for his family's history. He shared photos and documents about my grandfather and other family members. Conor is the grandson of Cahal Bradley my Granda's older brother, an extraordinary man. Cahal was a politician, journalist, novelist, and poet who was a leading member of Sinn Fein and was the first Nationalist Deputy Lord Mayor in the Derry City Council in 1920. In 1951 Cahal was elected to the Senate at Stormont as an Anti-Partition candidate. He had published two books. One, a collection of poems entitled 'Songs of a Commercial Traveler', the other 'Parishes of Ireland' a historical text documenting the history of Catholic parishes throughout Ireland. A remarkable third book entitled 'Next Stop Heaven' was sent to me by Conor. The book takes place in the Ardoyne district of Belfast in the late 19th century. It's a love story set in a backdrop of poverty, sectarian violence and emigration. Though this brilliant book was written in 1935, it sat as a family heirloom, unpublished and forgotten until Conor took the handwritten manuscript and had it published.

Which brings us to my Granda's manuscript, that I mentioned in the beginning of this now lengthy passage, and the book you have just read, and hopefully enjoyed. There were three copies of that manuscript, the one my mother had, and two carbon copies belonging to my Uncle Charlie which my mother took possession of upon his death, appropriately so, since she typed the manuscript for my Granda. I sent one copy off to Ireland for Conor to read. He loved it and encouraged me to publish it. Since the story is short, we both felt that it needed to be lengthened up a bit, but after numerous attempts by me to put in additional dialogue and story lines that did not seem to fit, I decided the story stands best on its own. It has a certain charm and style that should only be modified by the author. I hope, having read it, you agree with that decision.

Michael McDermott

September 2022

*Hugh and Charlotte (in forefront) and daughter
Margaret (fifth from left) in Ireland 1938*

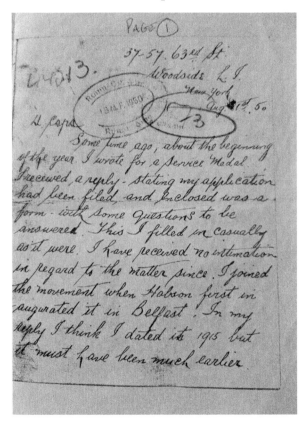

PAGE ①

57-57. 63rd St.
Woodside L.I.
New York
Aug 1st. 50

Some time ago, about the beginning of the year I wrote for a Service Medal. I received a reply - stating my application had been filed, and Enclosed was a form - with some questions to be answered. This I filled in casually as it were. I have received no intimation in regard to the matter since. I joined the movement when Hobson first inaugurated it in Belfast. In my reply I think I dated it 1915 but it must have been much earlier.

2.

I remember we held our meetings in
an office building in Royal Avenue.
E. McNeill became leader. There were
no designations as to rank. Those of us
who were the pioneers of the movement
especially in the North acted very much
on our own initative. I organised the
Volunteers in N. Belfast, Ardoyne
& Morrowbone. and for a time was
leader there, also I succeeded in
transforming the U. I. L. in those
areas into Young Ireland Movements
Our greatest problem was equipment
and I became a Clerk in the
British Ordnance in order to

3.

facilitate this important item.
Along with Boland Fitzgerald, DeValera
Coolan and others I helped to
organise the Volunteers in Tyrone
Down + Armagh. And when Young
Irelanders were few and far
between I acted as Volunteer
escort to Markievicz, Cahoon
DeValera, and others in dangerous
areas in Northern Ireland.
Throughout the struggle we had
many changes in rank, even after
G.H.Q. ceased being a floating
entity. For instance O Duffy came
to Belfast, but left in a very
short time. One should always

4.

bear in mind that the part of Ireland in which we pioneers struggled for freedom is not yet FREE. The whole story has yet to be written.

I think you & I met in Ballykinlar. And it is a pleasure for me to know that a man of your ability - is still serving our beloved Erin. I hope the time is not too far away when some of the glories of Ancient Erin will be resurrected in a New Parliament, preferebly on Tara's Hill, with every County represented by true Irish men.

Sincerely Yours.

Hugh Bradley

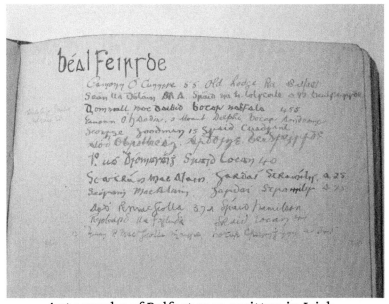

Autographs of Belfast men written in Irish - Ballykinlar Inernment Camp. Hugh sixth from top.

Ballykinlar Grafitti

Hugh (front row far right) with brothers Cahal (top center) and Francis (front row left) with Irish Republican Brotherhood associates.

FOR JOINING NEW FORCE.

ULSTER SPECIAL SHOT.

SUPPOSED ASSAILANT ARRESTED

Notices were recently posted on walls in the "Marrowbone" district of Belfast stating that any persons who joined the Special Constabulary would be shot.

An attempt to carry into effect the threat contained in the notices was made on Saturday evening, when a young Roman Catholic ex-soldier was shot at and wounded in the arm.

The victim of the affair was John Melough, who resides at 70 Chatham Street, Belfast.

The injured man joined the force on Thursday last, and had visited his home on leave. He was in uniform at the time, and was passing along Butler Street when he was attacked by four men.

Shots were fired by the assailants, who soon beat a hasty retreat. One of the bullets struck Melough in the arm, but fortunately did not cause a serious wound.

He was removed to the Royal Victoria Hospital, but was able to leave the institution after being treated.

Arising out of the incident the police have arrested Hugh W. Bradley, of 20 Herbert Street, Belfast.

The official report states :—

Special Constable J. Melough, while returning from Belfast to Newtownards Camp, at 6 p.m. on Saturday, was attacked by four men at the corner of Crumlin Road and Butler Street.

The men rushed at him, knocked him down, and while on the ground one of the attackers drew a revolver and fired, wounding him in the arm, but not seriously.

Rejection letter (a bit cold) from motion picture director John Ford. Hugh submitted the manuscript under the title 'Sinn Fieners Romance'.

Argosy Pictures Corporation
4021 Radford Avenue
North Hollywood, California

John Ford
CHAIRMAN OF THE BOARD
Merian C. Cooper
PRESIDENT

May 22, 1953

Mr. Hugh Bradley
3757 63rd Street
Woodside
Long Island, New York

Dear Mr. Bradley:

We are returning, enclosed, the manuscript
"A Sinn Feiners Romance", which you submitted to Mr. John Ford.

Mr. Ford's production plans are very in-
definite at the present time, and we are
not accepting any literary material.
We thank you for sending it.

Very truly yours,

John Ford Office

encl.

Apartment Building in Astoria Queens.
Home of the Bradley family in 1930

Empire State

By HUGH WILFRED BRADLEY

Issued by
National Manuscript Bureau
(SEE BACK COVER)

Empire State

by Hugh Wilfred Bradley

Copyrighted 1922 by Hugh Wilfred Bradley

The Belfast Convict Ship.

[COPYRIGHT]

A convict ship lies anchored, in Belfast Lough, to-day,
A symbol of the ancient times when gods were made of clay
The captives are from Ulster, brave men each one and all,
Who loved their native Erin, and responded to her call.
Through days of hellish terror, they strove by might and main
To bring that long-for freedom to Ireland once again—
Deprived the right to earn their bread, from daily toil made
    flee,
Their homes burned down, their churches wrecked—a pitiable
    sight to see,
And in the street in broad daylight—like blood hounds on the
    scent,
Tracked down by Orange mobs—to death they nobly went.

To them, each day, brought darker deeds — Cromwellian
    methods used—
Their children foully murdered—their women-folk abused;
The cruel foe, barbaric, killed babies at their play.
Oh, heavens! where's humanity—what has the world to say?
In Belfast streets the British troops stand heedlessly by
While homes are wrecked and looted—and even women die.
And Britain pays for all these crimes—her people one and all
Are aiding Craig in his foul deeds—by taxes big and small.
With armed Specials, paid and fed by England's cursed gold,
The Orange savage carries on—nor spares he young or old.

Centuries now are past and gone when strange ships at
    anchor lay,
In waters deep 'round Erin's coast, guarded night and day.
And in them brave men suffered hard that Ireland might live :
Oh heavens! how can we forget—aye, how can we forgive?
With Cromwell resurrected, the Orangeman rises high,
A figure of barbaric times and days long since gone by.
In North-East Ulster one can see cruel arts of long ago
Being put in use by demons great—a savage, heartless foe.
Beneath the cloak of England, Craig madly has his sway;
The world is blinded to the facts—but there will come a day !

Within that ship at anchor, brave men are suffering hard :
Irishmen! Unite, stand fast,—Liberty will be your reward.